MW01093987

ROOT ROT

SASKIA NISLOW

Creature Publishing
Charlottesville, VA

Copyright © 2025 by Saskia Nislow
All rights reserved.

ISBN 978-1-951971-25-0
LCCN 2024947132

Cover design by Luísa Dias
Spine illustration by Rachel Kelli

CREATUREHORROR.COM
🐦 @creaturelit
📷 @creaturepublishing

For Jamie

The Lake House was not on a lake at all, but a river. On the weekend we came to stay, the heavy spring rains brought it spilling into the overgrown backyard, where it pooled and settled, blanketing the bluegrass and clover in its mirror-black skin. At night, when we looked out our windows, the stars shone below us like seeds.

We were the children and grandchildren. Cousins. Though some of us were really uncles or nieces or something once removed. We called each other cousins. Nine altogether. Three threes. A magic number, someone told us. We don't remember who.

The House belonged to Our Grandfather. He had built it himself. This was what The Adults said whenever we expressed amazement at the fact that it was possible to have more than one house. Something about the way they said it made us sorry we'd asked. He'd put his blood, sweat, and tears into it, they told us. It was for us, for The Family, they said. The way they described it made it sound like Our Grandfather had built himself a larger body, one big enough for all of us to fit into.

According to The Adults, everyone used to come out to The Lake House once or twice a year, sometimes staying for only a few days and sometimes entire summers. They would drive boats out to where the actual lake was, only a mile or so down the road, and kayak around in the algae blooms. They would meet in the largest kitchen to cook enormous meals that they ate in the backyard as the bats skimmed insects out of the sky overhead.

That was a long time ago, though. The Oldest was the only one of us who had ever been, and that was when he was still just a baby. For over a decade, The Lake House stood empty.

Why did we come that year? None of us knew, not really. The Adults said it was to spend time together as a family again, like we used to. The Boy Twin said he heard that it was a sort of memorial to honor Our Late Grandmother. The Girl Twin disagreed. He didn't know anything about it, she claimed; he was just making it up to have something to say. The Liar said that Our Grandfather wanted to bring everyone together to decide who The House would go to when he died. None of us believed her.

The One Who Runs Away was picked up by an uncle from the train station a couple days early. The Twins and The Oldest, who lived closest, were driven up together with the rest of their families in a big van. The Baby, The Crybaby, and The Secret Keeper—all sisters—flew. The One with the Beautiful Voice did, too, but from somewhere else, and

The Liar took the bus up with her mother. The Others were already there.

As we traveled through the sparsely populated town where The House lived, our parents pointed out the parts that belonged to us in one way or another. It was hard to parse one patch of tree-studded land from another; it all seemed to belong together, but some of it had been sectioned off with invisible glass walls and marked ours. *What for?* we asked. The answers that came were vague, containing deceptively simple words whose hidden meanings only glinted at us: asset, invest, appreciate, develop.

We nodded like we understood and turned our attention to the green on green on green streaking across the car windows. And then, suddenly: the bright white paint of The Lake House.

Our legs stiff from traveling, those of us who got there early ran through the surrounding woods as everyone else trickled in, pine needles burrowing into our shoes and roots stubbing against our toes. By the time The One with the Beautiful Voice arrived with his father (around dusk, dinner getting cold in the big kitchen while we waited), we had gone so far in that we couldn't see the white of The House winking through the trees anymore. Behind the trees now stood more trees, like a mirror trick. Running felt like falling. We were falling in. The ground beneath us was covered up, hidden by the leaves and roots and needles and mushrooms and vines. The Baby, who we had placed there, dug into the debris.

Has she found it? we asked.

Did she find the ground?

Leaves crushed in her fat little hand, she stomped on a cluster of mushrooms and they exploded in a puff of smoke.

The mushrooms grew strangely there. Not in little crops or in lines, but in circles. We jumped in and out of them like they were hopscotch squares. We embellished their boundaries with pebbles and pine cones. We used them as "safety" when we played tag. The Baby's face and all our hands were covered in their dust. *Spores,* The Secret Keeper called it. We tried to get it off, scrubbing our palms with dead leaves and using spit to rub at The Baby's cheeks. We chased each other off into the trees, shrieking with laughter. Our voices circled each other higher and higher until they transformed into those of screaming animals. Running behind the trees, we looked like animals too.

Watch out for hunters, called The Girl Twin.

We look like deer.

And so we stopped, and brushed ourselves off and returned to the yard, and The Others joined us.

*

It was a big house. Bigger than any of us could have imagined. More like a museum of houses, a collection of different versions of the same rooms. There was the largest kitchen (all shiny white porcelain and cool steel), but there was also a green kitchen and a brick kitchen and a tiny, cramped yellow kitchen and, in the basement, a freezer that looked like a massive coffin and a jolly little refrigerator that The Adults said was just for drinks. There was a living room and a dining room and a sitting room and a dayroom and a TV room and a playroom and a library, and they were all different somehow, even though it seemed to us that they were all used for the same thing, which was sitting around. There were at least seven bathrooms, though there could have been more. The best one had a window in the ceiling right over the tub, and if we ran the water really, really hot, the steam filling the room pressed against the glass above us and it was like a cloud we could reach up and touch.

It would have been impossible to count all the bedrooms, but we didn't need to. The Adults, citing a need to decompress and "have some grown-up time," assigned us to a single section of The House, where we would be supervised by Our Young Aunt. "The Children's Wing" they called it, half ironically. Like a cherub, some of us thought. Like a hospital, thought others.

The Children's Wing was on the east side of The House, which of course meant nothing to us. To reach it, we either walked through a hallway on the second floor or entered through the back door, the one facing the river, and climbed up through a narrow brick stairwell. Our territory comprised the playroom, the TV room, the yellow kitchen, three bathrooms, and six bedrooms. Our parents were worried about dividing the rooms fairly, expecting that none of us would want to double up. The Twin's father loudly advocated that his children be allowed their own rooms.

"They always have to share," he barked, jabbing his finger into the air in front of Our Young Aunt's face.

The Baby's mother, who fretted over her daughters, cajoled The Secret Keeper to room with her sisters.

"Wouldn't it be a nice thing to do?" she wheedled. "Then your cousins can have their own rooms, and you can keep an eye on your sisters, and everyone will be so grateful to you."

The Baby's mother assumed, as we all did, that The Twins would share.

They needn't have worried. We didn't know if it was the whole house or just The Children's Wing, but there was an unsettled feeling to the air inside that made us not want to be alone. Tired of our own siblings, we instead partnered up by age and affinity. The Oldest and The One Who Runs Away quickly made themselves at home in the largest bedroom, the one the rest of us assumed would be taken by Our Young Aunt. They stretched their long legs out on top of the king-sized bed, their sneakers leaving streaks of forest floor on the linen duvet, their duffel bags and backpacks tossed carelessly over the antique vanity and carved oak armchair. The second largest room, and the only one with its own bathroom, was claimed by The Secret Keeper and The Girl Twin. The Liar tried to stay with them, too, pointing out that she could fit easily on the loveseat by the window, but of course this was deemed inappropriate. To stave off an argument, The Secret

Keeper took The Baby and stated decisively that the room was full.

Of the remaining rooms, two had double twin beds and two had singles. Our Young Aunt, who seemed slightly disoriented, most likely expecting to have been in one of the larger rooms with The Baby, took one of the singles. After some deliberation and a little whining, The Liar and The Boy Twin took one double, and The Crybaby and The One With the Beautiful Voice took the other. The remaining room stood empty, its door hanging open to the hallway, the mirror on the wall opposite reflecting us back at ourselves as we passed. We tried not to look.

*

Dinner that night was a trial; because of the late arrivals, the food sat out on the counter too long, turned lukewarm, started to congeal. None of us were used to eating in a big formal dining room. We squirmed uncomfortably in our too-hard chairs and kicked each other under the table. Our Grandfather set an extra place at the table, filling the plate there with steamed asparagus, mashed potatoes, roast chicken, and even a warm roll that he carefully buttered himself. We assumed this was for Our Late Grandmother, who passed the year before, which lent credence to The Boy Twin's theory about why we had come. It was right across from The Crybaby's seat, and she tried not to imagine her grandmother sitting across from her, pursing her burgundy lips disapprovingly at her meal.

To distract herself, The Crybaby tried to engage The Liar in a game of playing pretend, even graciously offering that they could both be fairies, or even princesses. But The Liar—who considered herself too old for that kind of baby game—had something else in mind.

I have a better idea, she whispered to her little cousin. *We can play Don't Look.*

The object of The Liar's game was simple: Don't look at Our Late Grandmother's chair. If you do, she'll look back at you. The Boy Twin, who overheard The Liar explaining the rules, decided to join in. Our Late Grandmother had not liked him much when she was alive. He was the type of boy that most adults saw as a pest—his interests too childish, his movements too aggressive, his voice too loud, too whiny. The idea of seeing her ghost scared him, and he liked to be scared.

The Crybaby did not like to be scared but saw no way to get out of playing the game. Now that The Liar had planted the idea in her head, she couldn't bring herself to look at the chair across from her. She tried to tell herself that The Liar was just being silly, that if she were to look across the table, the only thing she would see would be an empty chair and a place setting with the food untouched. When she imagined this, however, the empty space between the chair and table seemed to radiate a certain menace, like it hated her, like it *wanted* to scare her. She began to cry. The Secret Keeper, who was talking to The Girl Twin about private, older-girl things down on the other side of the table, heard this and, rolling her eyes, called her sister over to come sit with her. As The Crybaby walked the short distance between their two seats, she tried not to look at Our Late Grandmother's chair, while also trying not to intentionally *not* look. She cried harder.

The Liar and The Boy Twin continued their game. Without The Crybaby, it was a little less fun for The Liar, since all she had to do now was wait for The Boy Twin to look. She had no interest in looking. The game, after all, was her own invention. She watched her cousin carefully for signs of cracking. He picked at his asparagus, feigning concentration, and then turned to stick his tongue out at her. He was holding out for longer than she thought he would. She scanned the table to see if any of the rest of us looked bored enough to join. The Secret Keeper and The Girl Twin were comforting The Crybaby, who was still crying. The Oldest and The One Who Runs Away were doing something disgusting with the mashed potatoes that she normally might have been interested in if not for her game. The Baby, perched on Our Grandfather's lap, was gnawing enthusiastically on pieces of shredded chicken, and The One with the Beautiful Voice seemed to be in solemn conversation with one of the old cousins. Only one child sat alone. The Liar knew them; they were familiar to her, but it was a familiarity like when she accidentally caught a glimpse of herself in the mirror at night. Somehow both too distant and too intimate. Nameless. The child's head was bowed at an odd angle—tense, like something in their lap had startled them—and their hands were up by their face. Covering their mouth? Perhaps. There was no mouth to be seen. And she couldn't catch their eyes, though she could tell, somehow, that they were open.

With a jolt, she realized that she was looking at Our Late Grandmother's seat. She quickly counted the other children sitting around the table and then yanked on The Boy Twin's sleeve.

Look, she hissed.

She could feel the child across the table watching her but didn't look at it. The Boy Twin shrugged her off.

I'm not looking. He giggled, a little frantically. *You can't trick me that easily!*

She tugged harder and then, when he still didn't look up, grabbed his head in her hands and forced him to face it. He squeezed his eyes shut tight, and she tried to force them open with her fingers before hearing her name being barked from somewhere down the table. When she looked up, most of The Adults were staring at her and her mother was glowering. She let go of The Boy Twin.

We're just playing, he whined, though he wasn't even the one in trouble.

She muttered out an apology before someone forced her to, and The Adults all went back to their conversations. The Boy Twin turned to her.

What's your problem? he asked, though he wasn't really mad, only curious.

Look! she insisted again, not knowing what else to say. *There's someone sitting in Grandma's chair!*

The Boy Twin knew he was probably being tricked but looked anyway. He liked the way The Liar's words sent a thrill up the back of his neck. There was no one sitting there, though it looked, just for a split second, like there might have been. Not a person, though. The body didn't fit in the seat the right way. It was more like when his pointy old greyhound would jump up at the dinner table back at home and his mother would exclaim, "Boots thinks he's people!" It was gone before his eyes even registered it. A sort of mirage, perhaps, of the thing he thought *might* scare him.

There's no one there, he muttered. He had hoped to build up suspense to the point that even an empty chair might be a little thrilling, but now the game was ruined.

*

Once we were finished eating, The One with the Beautiful Voice volunteered to help clear the table. The rest of us resented this, as it meant we would have to pitch in as well or risk getting into trouble with our parents for embarrassing them. We scrambled for the easiest jobs—collecting napkins, gathering up the clean silverware. The One Who Runs Away, who tended to do things slowly, was stuck with clearing the dirty dishes to the kitchen, where Our Grandfather sat, overseeing it all. But he didn't seem to mind. Unlike The Others, he wasn't bothered by mess. He had just returned with the last remaining dishes when he thought to ask Our Grandfather what he should do with the food on Our Late Grandmother's plate. It felt wrong, somehow, to just throw it away.

"Do whatever you want with it," grumbled Our Grandfather from his perch on one of the old leather barstools.

A little scandalized, we turned back to The One Who Runs Away. As he reached toward the plate, we all noticed it at the same time: the food there had been eaten.

Immediately, our parents and aunts and uncles and even the old cousins descended upon us as one hissing, hollering mouth.

"Who did it?!" they cried.

"Which one of you was it? Come clean now and it'll be better for you later . . ."

"So disrespectful . . ."

". . . raised you better than this . . ."

"Is this how we taught you to behave?"

"Who was it? You can tell me. I won't say it was you that told."

None of us would cop to it. We didn't do it, we told them. It wasn't us. The Boy Twin offered the baffling suggestion that maybe a dog ate it, which no one paid much mind to as there weren't any dogs in The House. No one else had any ideas. The Adults deliberated for a little while—all except

Our Grandfather, who chatted with The One Who Runs Away about tax laws for rental properties, a topic none of the rest of us had any interest in—and decided that Our Young Aunt was to take us all back to The Children's Wing early, no dessert and no after-dinner time to play. Straight to bed.

Only The Boy Twin and The Crybaby protested. The One Who Runs Away shrugged, slipped a funny kind of bracelet made of knotted string Our Grandfather had handed him onto his wrist, and strode off to The Children's Wing with The Oldest trailing behind him. The One with the Beautiful Voice got kisses from the grownups, who assured him they knew it wasn't him, and then left with The Secret Keeper, The Girl Twin, and The Baby. Everyone expected The Liar to throw a fit or try to talk her way out of it. But she was quiet, distracted, gone before any of us even noticed.

*

Long after we were sent to bed, The Girl Twin woke abruptly from a half-sleeping nightmare. Half-sleeping because it had been somewhere between a dream and a hallucination; she was asleep, maybe, but her sleeping mind was in the same room she was in, seeing the same things she might have seen if she was sure her eyes had been open. Or at least, that's how it seemed to her at the time.

In the dream-room, the floor around her bed was crawling. Or, not crawling exactly. More of a rippling, shimmying motion. She couldn't tell if it was something on

13

the floor or the floor itself or both, but the creeping thing pulled itself off the floor and shuffled into bed with her. Tentatively, though, like a pet banned from sitting on the furniture. When it did this, she had—in her dream—tried to kick it off. She kicked and kicked and watched some sort of shade, like a dampness, slip down from the sheets and absorb back into the floor. But she couldn't feel anything against her feet except a thin, warm, skin-like membrane sticking to her toes like bits of tissue paper.

She woke up then. Or, at least, she opened her eyes. She could hear sounds from The Secret Keeper's bed. Sounds like breathing maybe, but not quite right somehow. The whistling sound it made reminded her of when gusts of wind blew in through the window. Open space to open space. Nothing filling up. For the briefest moment, she entertained the twilight thought that the shadow that had been on her bed had crawled under her cousin's covers and hid there. But that was silly. Still, she didn't look over at the other bed as she crept to the crib where The Baby slept, picked up the warm little bundle of blankets, and held it close.

*

That same night, while some of us dreamed, others stayed wide awake. The Oldest and The One Who Runs Away sprawled across their room, resentful at being sent to bed like much younger children, grumbling and eating their way through at least a quarter of the candy The One Who

Runs Away had stashed in his bag, dropping bits of chocolate onto the new white sheets, where they melted and glued themselves to the fibers.

They waited until The Baby stopped fussing and The Liar and The Boy Twin stopped giggling and Our Young Aunt stopped pacing the hallways and hissing "lights out!" Finally, when The Children's Wing was quiet and still, they cautiously tiptoed through the hallway toward the kitchen. As they passed the room at the end of the hall, they were startled by the door cracking open and The Secret Keeper's face poking out.

What're you two doing? she whispered. *Where are you going?*

The One Who Runs Away beckoned for her to join and, as she slipped out of her room and closed the door softly behind her, she saw that he was fiddling with that strange tangled bracelet Our Grandfather had given him at dinner.

And so, while the rest slept, the three oldest of us snuck into the kitchen and—after grabbing two bottles of amber liquid one of The Adults must have carelessly left in the cupboards and shoving them under our shirts—continued into the old stairwell where we crept down to the back door and then out into the waterlogged backyard, dragging the hems of our pajamas through the wet grass on our way to the forest.

The click of the door woke The One with the Beautiful Voice. Sleepily, he looked around the room for the sound's source before he caught sight of us out the window: The

Oldest, running ahead, only the glimpse of his bare foot visible before it slipped away into the tree line; The Secret Keeper and The One Who Runs Away talking together a few yards behind, and crawling behind them . . .

Well, not crawling exactly. It was a different sort of movement, but The One with the Beautiful Voice couldn't think of the word for it at that moment. He had thought, at first, that it was The Baby. It had looked just like her, so much so that he had started from his bed, ready to chase after her. But when he looked again, he realized his mistake. It wasn't The Baby at all. And perhaps it wasn't even crawling behind the rest of us, but in the opposite direction, back toward The House. Some kind of animal, maybe, though it didn't look like any animal he'd ever seen before. He stared harder at it, thinking, until he hit a realization and his short-lived fear dissipated. It was a blanket of some sort, or a scarf, blowing this way or that in the wind. It only looked like it was moving on its own. It only looked like something's skin.

*

The next morning, we were woken up by a loud banging. Tripping over our discarded outside clothes and fumbling with the door handles, we peered blearily into the hallway, where we were greeted by the sight of The Liar pounding on the door to Our Young Aunt's room. When Our Young Aunt finally opened it, squinting in her glasses, The Liar started yelling, though not at her, more like she had already been yelling about something and Our Young Aunt just happened to cross her path.

If my dad were here, he would kick their asses! she screamed, and we didn't know who she was talking about, but we all knew that wasn't true. No one liked The Liar's father, not even her mother. He opted out of family gatherings on her mother's side whenever possible, preferring to stay home and watch hockey on the couch instead of on his phone in the bathroom like he usually did. The rest of us heard our own parents talking about him in low tones sometimes, gossiping about how he made The Liar and her mother party to his own family's every whim and debating the benefits and drawbacks of "staying together for the children." To us, it didn't seem like The Liar cared much whether or not her parents stayed married, but maybe she was different at home. We all were. In our own ways.

"Language," Our Young Aunt chastised absently. The Liar continued as if no one had interrupted.

We gathered in the hallway to listen, all of us except for The Oldest and The Baby, who we assumed were still sleeping. From what the rest of us could tell, she was claiming that The Oldest and The One Who Runs Away had tormented her and The Boy Twin all night.

Didn't any of you hear? she wailed. *You must have heard them through your windows too!*

"Hear what?" asked Our Young Aunt.

You didn't hear them calling for us? You didn't hear the crying?

The rest of us shook our heads. The Boy Twin, standing next to The Liar, began to redden.

You kept calling and calling, The Liar insisted, directing her words now to The One Who Runs Away, who looked at her curiously, almost sympathetically.

And tapping on the window. I don't even know how you were doing that because every time we tried to look out, you would hide. You must have used a long stick or maybe you were throwing rocks. It went on for so long . . .

How did you know it was them? The Girl Twin asked her brother. *How do you know it was them when you say they hid every time you tried to see who it was?*

The Boy Twin, redder still, shrugged and then said defiantly, *Who else could it have been? And we obviously know what their voices sound like. Plus, we did catch him once.*

He pointed to The Oldest, who had just emerged from his room, rubbing his eyes blearily, the wrinkled imprint of the sheets still pink on his cheeks.

What're you two idiots even talking about? He yawned. *What is it you thought you saw? It definitely wasn't me. It was probably a squirrel or something.*

He and The One Who Runs Away laughed at this, though The One Who Runs Away's laugh didn't have much humor in it.

The Liar looked at The Boy Twin. We didn't know how to prove what we had seen, didn't know how to explain that, in the cavernous dark of the empty backyard at night, after we heard our names called to us in those same two voices in the same way we had heard them while playing together only hours before, there had been a flapping sound, like a lone pair of wings. Or perhaps just a single wing, beating the air by itself. And after this strange sound, we had seen something stranger still, fluttering by the submerged trunk of a skeletal birch, something we both recognized and did not.

We stared at The Oldest's face now but couldn't quite match it to what we had seen there, and our certainty waned.

I'm pretty sure we saw him or at least we saw something, The Boy Twin muttered.

The Girl Twin smirked at The Secret Keeper, who mouthed *boys* at her and rolled her eyes. The Girl Twin's conspiratorial smile wavered slightly.

I don't know what you guys are so smug about, The Liar cried, shriller by the second, her own face beginning to glow, *when you two were supposed to be watching your sister and they had her out there with them last night, using her for a stupid prank. We could hear her crying and crying the whole time and you didn't hear her at all? Not very resp—*

Shut uuuuup, one of us said, *stop lying. You sound stupid.*

The Secret Keeper rubbed her face in an exaggerated adult gesture of weariness and then stopped and seemed to listen for something.

Where is *The Baby?* she asked suddenly. *She's usually up by now. Did you see her in our room this morning? I don't know why I didn't check.*

This was directed to The Girl Twin, who shook her head.

I thought she was with you, The Girl Twin said. *Didn't you put her to bed last night? I thought she stayed with us. Did someone else come get her?*

We all looked at Our Young Aunt, who gazed placidly back at us.

"I haven't seen her," she said, not as worried—we thought—as she should have been. "I assumed one of you was with her. I haven't seen her since last night."

This kicked off another flurry of activity. Forgetting our momentary squabble (and ignoring the angry red splotches on The Liar's cheeks), we burst into The Secret Keeper's room. The Girl Twin, who was trying to remember if they had indeed had The Baby, checked the empty crib and then the floor near the hidden side of the bed. She couldn't quite recall what they had done the previous night for some reason. She could remember playing with The Baby right after dinner, and then could remember Our Young Aunt taking her to the large bathroom to give her a bath and get her ready for bed, but everything after that was strangely jumbled. She wasn't sure if The Baby had stayed with Our Young Aunt or had gone back to the room with us, where a crib was set up for her.

In the room, The Baby was nowhere to be found.

She wasn't in Our Young Aunt's room either or the main bathroom. We checked all the common areas, even opening the kitchen cupboards to see if she could've climbed in. The One with the Beautiful Voice, who felt guilty about everything even when he knew it wasn't his fault, started crying, which set off The Crybaby.

Shut up, hissed The Secret Keeper, who was just as confused as the rest of us and felt that, if anyone were to be crying, it should be her.

The Baby wasn't in the empty room, nor was she in the hallways or any of the hall closets. Even The Boy Twin, who had been grinning when this all started, relieved to no longer be on the outs with everyone, began to look scared.

We were just about to swallow our pride and go running to The Main House for The Adults when we heard crying coming from The Liar's room. We ran to it all at once, but The Secret Keeper got there first, casting her eyes about the space as another cry rang out, this one clearly coming from under The Boy Twin's bed. She crouched down and, reaching underneath, pulled out her sister. The Baby, who seemed tired and irritable, wrapped her arms around her older sister's neck and buried her face in her shoulder. Her diaper hung down almost to her knees and reeked of urine. The Secret Keeper laughed, though her expression remained worried.

Well, I guess that explains the mystery of who was keeping these guys up all night!

She held The Baby up high above her head and cooed at her.

Were you causing mischief? Were you bothering your cousins all night?

We all laughed and made fun of The Liar and The Boy Twin for making such a fuss over a yowling toddler.

The Boy Twin kicked the wall hard and ran to the bathroom, slamming the door behind him. We could see that he was crying and that made us feel a little sorry, but it also made us laugh harder. The Liar stayed with us, quietly stewing, and we respected her for that. Some of us even ruffled her hair a little as we went back to our own rooms to get ready for breakfast.

The only one who didn't join in the teasing was The Girl Twin, who leaned against the wall a little apart from the rest of us, wondering why no one else seemed to have noticed that The Baby's nails were caked with dirt.

*

The One Who Runs Away didn't join us for breakfast. He went out with Our Grandfather instead to run errands and check in on the new constructions. There was a lot Our Grandfather wanted to bid on, but some of the uncles weren't so sure, saying that it was too far from the water, too tucked away to be appealing to seasonal visitors.

"It won't be tucked away for long," was all Our Grandfather said, and from the uncles' faces we could tell it was settled. When he said this, The One Who Runs Away nodded seriously next to him like he was making the decision, too, which made us want to laugh and look away in equal measure.

He and The Oldest were the only ones asked to go with Our Grandfather and the uncles, he the only one who accepted. When we passed through the hallway that connected The Children's Wing to the rest of The House, some of us saw him waiting alone in Our Grandfather's big red pickup truck, the passenger's side door slightly ajar and one skinny, bare ankle emerging from the bottom corner and kicking back and forth over the drowned grass, creating two sets of ripples.

We fidgeted our way through eggs and bacon and toast with butter. When everyone was done, not even The One with the Beautiful Voice volunteered to help clean up. We wanted to explore. The Liar and The Boy Twin set off for the river immediately. The Girl Twin looked to The Secret Keeper to see what she wanted to do. She had a sense that The Secret Keeper knew more than she was saying about what had happened the night before. The Girl Twin silently cursed the now silly-seeming fear that had kept her from checking The Secret Keeper's bed when she woke in the middle of the night. Was it possible that some of the cousins snuck out? Would The Secret Keeper have joined? It didn't seem likely. And, even if that were the case, The Girl Twin didn't know why her cousin wouldn't have invited her along

23

or at least told her about it in the morning. The Secret Keeper was talking to The Oldest now and didn't look at her. A bit stung, and more than a bit embarrassed at feeling this sting, The Girl Twin followed her brother into the woods, and The Crybaby joined as well, half running to keep up. The Others stayed behind.

The four of us who went exploring followed the sluggish, puddle-like part of the river that flowed through the sodden backyard into the woods. None of us knew where we were going exactly, but The Liar walked with such confidence that we all followed her. The Twins walked next to each other on the path, catching up about their respective evenings, while The Crybaby followed awkwardly behind. She wanted to be a part of the conversation, but the crunching leaves made it difficult to hear. She was feeling out on the edges of things, as she often did with the older cousins, and couldn't figure out how to fit herself back in. She had been disappointed to see that there were no other girls in The Family around her age on the trip, unless she counted The Liar, which she wasn't sure if she did. Her older sister didn't, she knew, nor did most of The Adults save The Liar's mother, maybe, and a few of the aunts and the old cousins. But the rest of us seemed to, at least more or less.

The Liar, who was not thinking about these things and long past caring about who did what the night before, charged excitedly toward the deeper, faster parts of the river without looking back to make sure any of us were following her. In what she thought of as her real life, she lived with her parents in the city in a third-floor walkup that was far from parks or playgrounds. None of them liked it there; not permitted to play alone outside, The Liar spent a lot of time wandering through the apartment, trying and failing to find ways to entertain herself. Her mother said their neighborhood was "sketchy" and wanted to move them out to the suburbs, closer to where The Twins and The Oldest and some of the rest of Our Family lived. Her Father—though he made a big fuss about how obnoxious and ridiculous he found urbanites to be—seemed to be strangely overwhelmed by the pace of city life, made small by it, and wanted them to move farther north, where his own parents and siblings had been since he was a kid. The Liar often had the sense that her parents thought of the three of them together as incomplete somehow, half-separated from some larger whole, like a hangnail of a family.

Her own dissatisfaction mirrored theirs, but without an object to attach itself to. There was no other family, no lost comfort, to mourn. Instead, she had only the vague sense that things weren't as they were supposed to be, that there was a place—or a person maybe, or maybe just a feeling—waiting for her somewhere and she didn't know what or where it was but she could sense it pulling at her. Sometimes—like when she passed the twice-ridden, shiny red bike that hung in the hallway, rapidly becoming too small for her—this other thing seemed impossibly far away and out of reach. But out here, the possibility of it seemed to be in the very air around her, the very water rushing faster and faster beside her feet. She wanted to catch it.

The endless shushing of the river became louder and she knew she was getting close. After reading about them in school, she was desperate to make a dam. Something big, something that would flood the river even more, maybe up the front yard and all the way into the road. In her fantasy, the flood would destroy all exits and trap us at The Lake House, the water surrounding it teeming with dangerous animals like a castle moat. In this fantasy (which she knew was silly and would never tell another living soul about), The Adults were never included. Where had they gone? She couldn't say, didn't think much about it. But the rest of us all stayed together. So close together that it was hard to tell when one of us ended and the other began. Closer than close. So close we couldn't have even recognized each other.

When she finally reached the deepest part of the river, she marveled for a moment at its size and the way its borders seemed to bleed into the forest floor. Grass and foliage poked out of the water near the edges, and even a few small trees were partially submerged, their roots rising from the surface like the backs of some strange aquatic creatures. The Liar began gathering branches and leaves for the dam, looking eagerly back at the path for the rest of us to arrive.

Before we could get there, however, she was distracted by a rustling sound in the woods across the river. When she looked up to locate it, she saw some movement by a cluster of weeds surrounding the rocks that lined the bank. She began removing her shoes to wade across when something leapt from the weeds and perched in the shadow of the largest boulder. She couldn't make it out exactly, other than the rough shape of it, but it was small, perhaps a bit larger than a squirrel. It wasn't the shape of a squirrel, though. It was more like a very small person whose body was designed to walk on all fours. A fox perhaps? She didn't know what foxes looked like outside of cartoons. How big were they supposed to be? She began making her way through the rushing water, clawing her toes around the algae-slicked rocks and trying to balance her slight weight against the relentless river pounding. Her splashing footsteps seemed to startle the creature, and it jumped from the shadow and into the tall grass surrounding the river and vanished. She was able to catch only a quick glimpse—a flap of pale skin, something like fingers but arranged differently—and then it was gone.

She tried to follow, going so far as to check the ground for tracks, but it'd left no trace. There were footprints in the muddy ground, but not ones made by an animal. The person who made them must have been small, smaller even than The Liar herself. She followed them into the forest. As she traveled deeper in, the trees became thicker and darker, like lines of a spiral crowding in on themselves as they moved toward the center. She was dimly aware of our voices calling out behind her, but paid them no mind, stopping only when the tracks terminated at the foot of an enormous leafless tree.

There were no tracks on the other side of the tree or nearby. The Liar knelt, curious, searching for where the person making them might have gone. It was difficult to determine within the roots what was a curve and what was a burrow and what was something else. Most of the tunnels or openings were too small for anything larger than a rabbit to fit through, in The Liar's estimation at least. She stepped over the soft-skinned mushrooms ringing its base and braced herself against the great gray trunk, trying to get a better vantage point, when the ground beneath her seemed to give and her foot pushed through the rot up to the ankle. Stumbling, she knocked her knee hard against a boulder and then righted herself.

Her foot had made a sizable dent in the tangle of roots, causing a deep split in one of the largest. Through the opening, she could see something that didn't look like it was part of the tree. She pulled at the damp, ragged bark edges and found that the wood gave way easily, almost disintegrating in her hand. As she dug deeper into it, her fingers brushed against something that was soft in a different way. Like rubber almost, or skin. She pulled her hand away quickly, sure she had touched a sleeping animal. But nothing moved within the hole. She tentatively reached inside again and realized that the thing was cold, yielding, and moist, not like skin at all. Though her hands were raw and her nails dirt-caked, she scraped and clawed around, pulling away chunks of half-digested forest floor until she finally exposed the thing inside.

*

The Liar's scream carried through the trees to the river that those following behind her were still struggling to cross. And then farther, past the wood shakes lining the roof of The Lake House, over the gutters clotted with twigs and moss, and then down down down into the dirt. This is where some of us heard it, so faint it didn't even sound like a scream at all, but like something whispered just to us. Like a secret.

*

Back at The House, The Secret Keeper sat with The Oldest on the Adirondack lawn chairs on the hilly, dry part of the yard, talking about the events of the morning while The One with the Beautiful Voice played with The Baby in the grass.

I feel a little bad, The Secret Keeper said, laughing to herself self-consciously. *I mean, they weren't wrong that you two—that we—were out there.*

It's just a coincidence. You were there with us so you obviously know they were lying, The Oldest said, picking at the rotting arm of his chair.

Of course, The Secret Keeper replied. *But I do wonder if maybe they heard us or something and got confused. And then all of us acted like they were crazy. I mean, it's their own fault of course, for making up stories for attention like they always do . . .*

What she didn't say was that she hadn't been with the two of them the whole night. The Oldest had run ahead of them when they got out into the yard, had run ahead of them both, calling back that he was going to drink all the liquor himself, egging them on to chase him. Though part of her wanted to, The Secret Keeper could never quite bring herself to do what she thought of as childish things without feeling embarrassed. It seemed right for other people her age to behave this way, but not her. Whenever she tried to act carefree or silly, she felt like a pretender. And so, as The One Who Runs Away and The Oldest chased each other into the woods, The Secret Keeper stood just outside the edge of the tree line, waiting for them to come back. It took a long time, long enough that she had started to get worried, but then the other two emerged and we all walked down to the lake together.

I mean, who knows if they heard us or not, but if anyone should feel guilty about confusing those two, it's whoever was supposed to be watching The Baby. It wasn't you, right?

The Secret Keeper looked at The Oldest. His face was turned mostly away from her as he spoke with an uncharacteristically flat affect, almost droll. This was unusual for him. Though he was the oldest of us, he was the youngest in his immediate family by nearly a decade and acted it. The Secret Keeper had noticed this change in demeanor since our time in the woods last night. She didn't like to think she might have been left out of something, but wondered if he and The One Who Runs Away had shared some secret the night before that she wasn't privy to, one that made them more grown-up somehow. The thought of this made her uncomfortable.

No, The Secret Keeper murmured, embarrassed. *No, she was supposed to be with . . . someone else. One of them was supposed to be watching her. I can't remember . . .*

She tried to think. There was a quality to this conversation that reminded her of when her mother would tell her about the trip The Family took to Ireland when The Secret Keeper was just an infant. Her mother talked about this trip all the time and liked to show photos to all of her daughters, even though two of us hadn't even been there. The one particular photo that The Secret Keeper liked of herself was the one where she sat, wrapped in a bulky sweater, on her father's lap in the wet grass by the edge of a great ocean cliff. When she looked at it for a long time, she could smell the damp wool and the ocean spray, could feel the chill of the day and her father's stubbly chin resting against her cheek. But she had no idea if she really remembered these things or just imagined them from looking at the picture so often.

Similarly, though she remembered leaving The Lake House with the knowledge that her sister was sleeping safely in her crib, something else nagged at her. There was another memory. Or a fantasy of a memory. In this fantasy, before she had joined us in sneaking out, she noticed that The Baby was awake and standing up in her crib. Not wanting her sister to make a fuss, she had picked her up and carried her out with us. And when we had crossed over the wet grass, she had dangled The Baby over it, tickling her feet, and we had all laughed about it together. When her mind snagged on this fantasy, she could almost feel The Baby's soft little hands holding onto her thumbs. But only almost.

One of them should've been watching her.

In her peripheral vision, she could feel The Oldest watching her. As she turned to check his expression for doubt, she experienced a momentary, dizzying vision in which his face appeared to be torn, the part of it closest to her intact, but a ragged edge running from the opposite eyebrow down to the corner of his set mouth, and then nothing but the cataract sky behind him. Then he smirked at her and the features of his face seemed to snap back into place. Just a trick of the light.

At their feet, The One with the Beautiful Voice rested his cheek against the cool ground and made faces through the grass at The Baby, who wanted to play peekaboo. If he squinted just right, it looked like the ground was a small, bustling city, like the kind in his Richard Scarry books. The Baby squealed with delight and babbled at him incomprehensibly. Only a year or so ago, he might've been able to understand her; his own sister was only a couple years older than her, and when she was just an infant, he used to translate what she was saying to his parents. Much to his disappointment, his sister—in a clingy stage—had stayed home with his mother, who was pregnant again and said that the trip would be too much for her.

He liked playing with toddlers well enough, but he was disappointed that The Crybaby—his only real friend on the trip—had chosen to go with The Others to the river. He hadn't expected her to; he thought she, like him, would want to do something quiet and solitary. The night before, as Our Young Aunt paced the hallways, they had discussed making a fort in the empty room, one just for them that no one else was allowed into.

His thoughts were interrupted by the sound of someone calling for him over the breeze. It was difficult to determine where it was coming from, and he scanned the yard to locate an adult but found no one. The call came again and he stood, straining to hear. Off the ground, he was able to identify the old shed across the yard as the source of the sound. He kissed The Baby quickly on the forehead and, after checking to make sure the other two had an eye on her, set off in search of the person calling his name.

The shed, which was slightly hidden in the tall grass of the yard and the shadow of The Children's Wing, was in poor condition. There remained only the barest hint of red paint on the rotting boards, and the metal details on the door were rusted past orange and into a sort of licheny brownish-green color. Mushrooms ringed the entire structure, interwoven with weeds growing high enough to obscure the lower parts of the windows, and it was into these weeds that The One with the Beautiful Voice peered, searching for a familiar face. When he finally reached the shed, walked around the perimeter, and found no one outside, he grudgingly approached the door and—with some effort—wrenched it open.

In the dim light inside, he saw a figure with its back turned to him. It was hard to make out who it was. He knew it was one of us, an older boy, but which one he couldn't say.

Were you calling my name? The One with the Beautiful Voice asked.

The older boy didn't turn around immediately. Instead, he continued fiddling with something on the drafting table that The One with the Beautiful Voice was too small to see. The One with the Beautiful Voice repeated himself, a little quieter, but the figure seemed to hear him this time. He finally turned and The One with the Beautiful Voice saw that it was The Oldest. He didn't know how it was possible that he hadn't recognized him when he had seen him just moments before or how he didn't notice his older cousin leaving the yard, but he also felt a sense of relief that this was just a continuation of the time they were spending together. Just a new game.

There you are, The Oldest said, smiling. There was something strange about his face that The One with the Beautiful Voice couldn't quite make sense of. Something missing, maybe. It made him nervous. *I have something I think you'll want to see.*

You do? whispered The One with the Beautiful Voice. *What is it?*

It's down by the lake, his cousin replied as he started to move closer. *I found it when I went there this morning. It's a really special sort of thing, hard to describe.*

The One with the Beautiful Voice didn't know what to say, so he just nodded.

I wonder if you could help me make sense of it, The Oldest continued. *You seem like you're really smart, like you might know things I don't.*

The One with the Beautiful Voice was flattered, but he did not want to see it. Though perfectly comfortable with adults, he was uneasy around older children and didn't much like playing outside unless it was at one of the nice playgrounds near his house or somewhere else he was used to and thought of as safe. But he couldn't figure out how to say no politely.

Okay, he said. *I don't know if I'll be very helpful, but I can look.*

The Oldest grinned and, for a moment, his features seemed to slide a little apart, to tilt so that they were facing the wrong direction.

Climb on my back. I'll carry you there.

I can walk, said The One with the Beautiful Voice. *It's okay. I can walk.*

Climb on my back.

And so The One with the Beautiful Voice climbed onto his cousin's back. The Oldest walked to the door and then through it and, as we left, The One with the Beautiful Voice could see what his cousin had left on the workbench. It was a short length of rope, kinked like it had been worked into knots and then untied.

As we moved outside, The One with the Beautiful Voice was surprised to see that the rest of us were gone from the yard. The House, too, seemed empty, and he could no longer hear the adult conversations from inside. He wondered where everyone had gone off to and began to worry that he had been in the shed somehow longer than he thought. The sun before had been hidden by the milky skin of morning fog, but now the outside seemed strangely dark, as if the sun weren't hiding anymore but had vanished. Suddenly very tired, he rested his head on The Oldest's shoulder and, as the older boy began to whistle a strange melody, fell gently asleep.

*

By the time the rest of us reached her, The Liar was so hysterical that we couldn't work out what exactly she was upset about. The Crybaby burst immediately into sympathetic tears.

Stop acting like a girl. Are you going to explain what's wrong or are you just going to make a scene? hissed The Girl Twin. As she said it, she knew her words threatened to ruin their fun together, but she hated when other people cried in front of her. She knew that this wasn't good of her, but she couldn't get past her discomfort at the sight of tears and so usually settled on trying to get them to stop by whatever means necessary, even if it meant being a little cruel.

Yeah, added The Boy Twin, eager to ally himself with his sister. *Stop being such a baby.*

The Liar started up with a fresh wail. It took several minutes to calm her down enough that she was able to speak clearly, during which time The Girl Twin felt herself growing both increasingly frustrated and increasingly guilty about this frustration.

The Baby, The Liar gasped out finally. *She's in the tree.*

We followed her gaze to a hollowed-out section at the base of a half-rotten tree. The Boy Twin started laughing but stopped when he saw his sister didn't join in with him. The Liar caught his eye and held his gaze for a long moment.

Look for yourself, she said, and then walked a bit away to go sit on a boulder with her face in her hands.

The Twins told The Crybaby to go sit with her, which she did without complaint. We tried to peer into the dug-out part of the roots but found that there was too much rot and debris to gain a clear view. There was something in there, though. Something sort of a warm whitish-gray color, soft looking. Mold perhaps, thought The Girl Twin with an odd shiver. That would explain it.

The Boy Twin, who hoped that The Liar had found something gross, began digging into the soft wood, tearing chunks of rot away in handfuls. He stopped when his hands hit something soft and clammy.

There's something in there, he whispered to his sister. *It feels like skin.*

As we worked together to clear away enough wood that whatever was in the roots of the tree could be extracted, The Girl Twin was reminded of a time when there was a family of mice living in the walls of her house. They tore through the cupboards, leaving chewed-through plastic and droppings everywhere. After a few half-hearted attempts with no-kill traps, her mother—a self-professed animal lover—simply gave up.

"I guess we'll just have to find a way to live together!" she'd said with a shrug.

The Girl Twin resented this. She was disgusted by the now-filthy kitchen cupboards, and the scrabbling of the mice's feet kept her up all night. She couldn't understand how her mother could act as if nothing was the matter, as if nothing could be done about it. Her father, who was rarely home but whom she passionately admired, always said that you had to face your problems head-on. Otherwise, he warned, they'd snowball out of your control.

And so when The Girl Twin wrapped her hands around the soft shape caught in the rot, she tried not to think about what she was actually doing and instead remembered how it felt to open up the snap traps she had set for those mice, how their heads wobbled a little when she lifted the metal holding down their necks, how their cold, wormy tails felt between her fingertips as she carried them outside to throw in the next-door neighbor's trash bins. It had been a satisfying feeling, like she had just cut something rotten off her own body.

*

It did look like The Baby, The Boy Twin thought as he examined the thing his sister had pulled from the tree. But it wasn't exactly The Baby. It couldn't be. At first glimpse, he thought that The Liar was right, that it was her. His sister had screamed when she saw what she was holding and had dropped it to the ground, and then he had screamed, too, and then both went deadly silent. But, after a few awful moments, he was able to bring himself to look closer, and there he saw that no, it couldn't have been The Baby at all because it wasn't a person. What he had initially taken to be dead flesh was actually some sort of mushroom or fungus. It covered the form (which was shaped, he had to admit, much like The Baby, all the way down to her little fingers and toes, her thin hair that wasn't quite long enough to pull up into a ponytail) and grew so thick that, when he finally gathered the courage to touch it, to try to push it aside to see what was underneath, he could only find more of the stuff. The fungus was white with occasional patches of gray and tan. It grew in little spun-sugar clusters and tiny stalks no thicker than a piece of spaghetti with rounded little caps on the top that could barely be seen unless you looked very closely. The stalks seemed to sway a little, even though the air was completely dead, not even the slightest breeze passing through. A few of the mushrooms were a bit larger—two with slimy caps where The Baby's eyes might have been, a line of them like teeth by the place where her mouth should be. The Boy Twin pushed at one of the "eyes" and then drew back his hand at the feel of it.

What the hell, he whispered.

The Girl Twin, who had been watching all of this from a slight distance, finally approached the thing and looked at it carefully, pushing her finger hard into where The Baby's stomach might have been.

What do you think's under there? she asked.

I don't know, replied the Boy Twin. *It just looks like more mushrooms to me.*

We should check, said The Girl Twin. *Just in case, we should check before we tell them anything.*

She flicked her eyes over to the two of us who were still crying over on the rocks.

The Boy Twin nodded.

Okay, he said, eager to prove his own bravery after his sister was the one to take the thing out. *Okay, I'll do it.*

He crouched back down and, taking a deep breath, sunk his hands into what could have been the thing's mouth. The fungus seemed to be able to fold into itself endlessly, becoming tougher and tougher the harder he pushed into it. He tried to grab a handful and pull, but the stuff was too slippery and slid right out of his grip. He scraped at it with his fingernails but couldn't get much up. Frustrated, he searched around and located a sharp stick, which he stabbed hard into the place where the thing's chest would be. There was a slight, momentary resistance, and then the stick punctured it with a soft *thunk*. Grasping the end of the stick hard with both hands, he pushed down further and then pulled it toward him as hard as he could. With resistance, the stick dragged several inches through the thing before snapping apart in his hands. From out of the puncture sprang thick droplets of a deep red liquid. Shaking slightly, he pulled the gash apart as wide as he could and looked in. More white mushroom flesh, now bubbling with red.

What do you see? The Girl Twin asked, sounding nauseous. *Is there anything underneath?*

It's just more mushrooms, he answered. *I don't know what this red stuff is but it's just more mushrooms. There's nothing else inside.*

*

Somewhere, we felt the pain of the stick digging into us. Not the real pain but the memory of it, of what it would have felt like. That was what made it hurt so much.

*

By the time The Secret Keeper noticed that The One with the Beautiful Voice wasn't playing in the grass with The

Baby anymore, the light had turned oily and thick as the fog cleared and the sun sagged lower in the sky. It seemed later than it should have been. Somehow, we had all missed lunch. None of The Adults had come calling for us. She had a vision of her younger cousin wandering away toward the old shed, but it didn't seem like a real memory. In her real memory, The One with the Beautiful Voice had been with us only moments before. And then he was gone.

Did you see him leave? she asked. *I could've sworn he was just here.*

The One Who Runs Away, who was sitting in the chair next to her, shook his head. The Secret Keeper looked over at him and had the odd feeling that he wasn't supposed to be there but couldn't figure out why.

I think he wandered off a while ago, he said. *Into the woods. Both of them did. You didn't notice?*

At first, she thought he meant The Baby. She looked around for her sister, sure for a moment that she would be gone, and was relieved to find her playing peekaboo by herself in the grass, hiding her face and revealing it to no one. The Secret Keeper stood to go search for the rest of us when Our Young Aunt poked her head out of the window.

"Is everything okay?" she called down from The Children's Wing.

We waved at her and nodded.

We're just playing a game! yelled The One Who Runs Away. *Hide-and-seek!*

42

Our Young Aunt nodded and closed the window.

Should we go look for them? The One Who Runs Away asked. There was a certain weariness in his voice that took The Secret Keeper by surprise.

Yeah, probably, she replied. *How were errands this morning, by the way?*

The One Who Runs Away shrugged, but The Secret Keeper caught the pride in his eyes when she asked.

He just wanted to show me what he and the guys have been working on. You know, the houses next door that they're fixing up. It's a big job. Kinda crazy that he's taking it on right now, but he is *really healthy for his age, I guess. Anyway, I'm just glad I can help out. I don't know if your dad told you about any of this stuff. I'm sure it'd probably be really boring to you, but I'm kinda into it.*

I don't think it's boring, The Secret Keeper replied, stung. She had in fact been hoping to be invited. Her father was proud of his role in this new venture, an offshoot of the long-standing family contracting business, and would sometimes talk to her about which wood samples had the highest quality for the best price and other things of that nature. Since The Secret Keeper was young, she had always been talented at drawing, and lately, her mother had been encouraging her to ask one of the uncles to teach her how to draft blueprints.

It's just really cool of him to include me in this stuff even though my parents pretty much never bring me to visit, The

One Who Runs Away concluded, a little bitterly. The Secret Keeper hadn't realized he was still talking.

The light was starting to dim outside, and we were sure The Adults would begin calling us in for dinner at any moment, so we decided to head into the woods to find The Others. The Secret Keeper bent down to pick up The Baby and found it difficult to lift her. Somehow, she must have been holding onto the ground so hard that she felt almost rooted there. She looked to The One Who Runs Away for help but he was distracted, fiddling with the bracelet he'd been wearing since yesterday. It reminded her of the bracelets she and her friends had made each other when she went to sleepaway camp, all the different knots and braids and color combinations she had so diligently learned. This bracelet lacked any of that skill or care, though. It was more like the way The Secret Keeper used to tie her shoelaces when she was little. Knot after knot after knot to make sure they wouldn't come undone. She tugged again and finally managed to wrench her sister from the ground. We set off into the trees.

*

The Baby insisted on walking, so progress through the forest was slow. The One Who Runs Away banged a stick against the trees as he called for The Others. After he whacked one sapling so hard it split in half, he heard The Secret Keeper's footsteps stop behind him.

There was something in the trees! she whispered. *Did you see?*

Why are you whispering?

She made a face at him and pointed to what she saw, off the path and deep into the woods where the trees grew branchless for dozens of feet into the air. It was hard to make out, but it looked almost as if a figure were standing among the foliage, standing very still. She wasn't quite sure if it was actually a human being, though, or simply an odd-shaped tree.

Look. Over there. I think it might be a person.

She pointed it out to The One Who Runs Away, who looked hard in the direction she indicated.

I don't see anything.

There, by the bent tree.

She strained to see better. Everything in the forest looked like everything else. Trees behind trees. She crept toward it as quietly as possible. It did look like a person. A small person, The One with the Beautiful Voice maybe, turned so he was facing away from her and holding himself perfectly still. She remembered what The One Who Runs Away had told Our Young Aunt. Were we all playing hide-and-seek and she had just forgotten?

Do you think that's him? she whispered to The One Who Runs Away. She felt silly whispering, but there was a strange quiet in the air that put her on edge.

I can't tell, replied The Oldest, who was suddenly next to her. *I don't know what he's doing if it is him, though.*

She looked to The One Who Runs Away and then back at The Oldest. The two boys looked at each other and seemed to exchange a smirk.

I thought . . . she started.

Naw, I just went to go check out the shed while you guys were talking. I don't know where he went. Probably to go find The Others, I'm guessing.

She was unnerved by his nonchalance and couldn't get a read on The One Who Runs Away's feelings about all this. More and more, her grasp on what was happening seemed to be slipping away from her. She squinted again at the figure, which she was now fairly certain *was* a figure and not just a strange tree. It was around The One with the Beautiful Voice's size and shape. Small, even for seven, with spindly arms and legs and shoulder blades so sharp they could be seen through his shirt. He was hunched forward with his head bowed, sort of a grayish hue all over, but she couldn't tell if that was just due to the weakening evening light. There was an arm, or something like it, twisting out from behind his back like he was reaching out toward her. For some reason, she was hesitant to call out to him unless she could be sure it was her little cousin. She focused on the hair. The One with the Beautiful Voice, she knew, had wavy hair that curled around in a spiral cowlick at the back of his head. If she could just make out the hair, she thought, then she would know it was him and could give him a talking-to about scaring people for no reason.

She stared hard at the back of the figure's head, trying to make out what the hair looked like. It did seem like there was a sort of swirl pattern there. Yes, right there. As she scrutinized it, it started to come into clearer focus: a dark whorl in the center twisting everything else around it. But not like hair at all. No, it was just a strange empty space. Like a sinkhole, thought The Secret Keeper. She blinked and tried to look away and then stopped suddenly.

He was looking at her.

He hadn't turned, but he was looking at her. She was sure of it. She could feel it, could see it, not even eyes exactly but something else that her own eyes couldn't make sense of.

Let's go, she whispered, barely audible, already starting to back away as fast as she could without making too much noise. *It's not him. Let's get out of here. I don't like it.*

But The Oldest was distracted, peering intently at something behind them on the other side of the trail.

What? he responded, loudly. Too loud.

The Secret Keeper was practically back to the path now. The figure seemed to be walking backward toward her, so quickly that its feet weren't moving at all. Like a fan spinning faster and faster until the blades freeze. How could The Oldest not see it?

Let's go! she hissed. *It's not him!*

The Oldest laughed.

What? Are you scared of a tree? Here, I'll go check it out for you. You're gonna feel so stupid when you see it.

As she stumbled back onto the path, he began walking toward the figure at a mock leisurely pace, looking back at her to check her response. In front of him, the figure drew closer, though he didn't seem to notice. There was something wrong with its feet, The Secret Keeper realized. They didn't fit together with its legs in the right way. If only she had noticed it sooner, she thought wildly, everything could've been okay. They could've been safe.

It reached The Oldest before he reached it. Or, at least, that's how it looked to The Secret Keeper, though she wouldn't have been able to explain what that meant had anyone asked her. He looked back at her and then turned toward it. The figure was no longer moving at all. There was not even, The Secret Keeper realized, the rise and fall of shoulders to indicate breath. She watched as The Oldest reached his hand up as if to pat it on the head. The spiral there seemed to open wider as his hand approached, slowly engulfing his fingers, then the entire hand. Not as if it were eating him, but more like his body was disappearing *into* it, becoming a part of it. He didn't seem to notice.

Stop! The Secret Keeper cried when she finally found her voice.

The Oldest looked back at her curiously and, when he did so, she was certain there was another figure there, too, one just his size, standing back-to-back with him. She blinked and the vision was gone.

What're you freaking out about? It's just a tree. See?

And as he waved his hand in front of the dark burl on

the tree's trunk, the place The Secret Keeper had been sure just moments ago was a mouth, she saw that he was right. It was just a tree. An old, half-dead tree covered in graying bark and patches of almost colorless moss. She didn't know what she could have possibly been thinking before.

Are you guys coming?

The One Who Runs Away had almost disappeared around the corner ahead of us and we half ran to catch up with him.

*

When the oldest cousins finally reached us, The Crybaby was done crying. The Girl Twin sat next to her on the ground, her arm wrapped around her cousin's shoulders a little too tightly.

Don't be stupid, she hissed. *Don't be a baby. See? It's not anything scary. Calm down. Stop making a fuss.*

The Crybaby sniffed and wiped her nose on the sleeve of her shirt. The Liar and The Boy Twin stood above them stoically, staring at a brutalized mass of mushrooms oozing red liquid onto the ground.

What's wrong? The Secret Keeper cried as she came crashing in through the trees. *Is everything okay? What happened to her?*

The Girl Twin looked up at her cousin, simultaneously relieved to have help and disappointed that now the promise of fun truly had slipped away from her. There would be no playing in the river with her brother and The Liar. There would be no mess, no carefree silliness. It was time to be responsible.

She's fine, The Girl Twin muttered. *She's just being hysterical.*

No, she's not, snapped The Liar, drawing her eyes away from the mushrooms for the first time.

Both The Oldest and The Secret Keeper looked confused.

The Liar elbowed The Boy Twin hard in the side. The Girl Twin glared at both of them. The Crybaby sniffled.

It's not really a big deal . . . began The Boy Twin, trying to find a way to please both his sister and The Liar, and instead pleasing neither of them. *We just found something in the tree. It was kind of weird, but it's not serious. She just got scared, that's all.*

We also found something in the trees, murmured The Secret Keeper, though too quietly for anyone to hear her clearly.

The Girl Twin looked at her sharply.

What did you say?

But The Secret Keeper ignored her. *What did you find that was so scary?* she asked, kneeling to be eye level with her younger sister in a way that made it clear that no one else should answer for her.

The Crybaby whimpered dramatically, and The Boy Twin rolled his eyes and kicked at the bleeding clump of mushroom.

What is that? The Secret Keeper asked.

The Crybaby started to cry again. The rest of us all stumbled over each other trying to explain. Eventually, The Boy Twin, who was the loudest, won out.

We found it in the trees! There's something wrong with it. It looked like The Baby . . . we thought it was her at first, but I guess it's not. But it looked like her. And it's bleeding! There's something wrong with it. It's gross.

The One Who Runs Away knelt to take a look at the mushrooms. The Oldest stepped back and looked bored.

The Secret Keeper laughed then and stood up, brushing the dirt off her knees.

Oh, those mushrooms? There's nothing wrong with them. I read about them in a book one time. "Bloody tooth" mushrooms, I think they're called. Or something like that. It's not blood, anyways, just ooze. It's nothing to be worried about. And The Baby is fine! She's . . .

The Secret Keeper trailed off as the rest of us listened intently. The Oldest put his hand on her shoulder and a strange blank expression passed over her face for a moment. She shook her head.

She's back at The Lake House with The Others.

Oh man, she said, turning to The Oldest and laughing in a nervous sort of way. *I completely forgot that he took her back to the house. Why did we think he was missing? We watched him leave with her.*

She turned back to the rest of us to explain about The Baby and The One with the Beautiful Voice. By this point,

The Crybaby, realizing that no one was paying attention to her anymore, had stopped crying and was prodding around the clump of mushrooms with a stick, gathering the courage to try to touch it.

Sorry, The Secret Keeper started, trying to explain to us in a way that would make sense that she and The Oldest had been looking all over for The One with the Beautiful Voice even though they had watched him take The Baby inside. *I don't know what's wrong with me. I guess it just slipped my mind. I feel like an idiot.*

Everyone laughed, but there was still a strange energy in the air. A loud crack broke the tension, and we looked over to see that The One Who Runs Away had snatched the stick out of The Crybaby's hands and snapped it in half.

Leave it alone, he muttered, his face turning red.

The Crybaby, shocked, just gaped at him. She had just wanted to try to touch it like everyone else did. She wanted to be brave enough. Why was everyone so mean to her? She looked to her sister to see if she was going to say anything about it, but The Secret Keeper still seemed to be lost in thought.

I'm not going crazy, right? she asked, turning to The Oldest. *They're back at the house, right? We just forgot?*

The Oldest shrugged. *Yeah, I mean that's what I remember. I thought you saw something else.*

The Girl Twin stood up and helped The Crybaby to her feet. *Well, alright. Everyone's okay then. We should probably head back for dinner. It's getting late.*

We brushed the dirt and dead leaves from our jeans and the palms of our hands, then filed down the path back toward The House. The Secret Keeper and The Girl Twin took the lead, with The Crybaby on their heels and The Oldest and The Boy Twin following close behind. The Liar, who had to tie her shoelaces, noticed that none of us waited for her. Even The One Who Runs Away, who lagged behind with her, wasn't paying her any attention. Instead, he picked up the decimated clump of mushrooms, cradling it tenderly like it really was the child we had taken it to be, and gently placed it back within the rotten burrow at the base of the tree.

*

The One with the Beautiful Voice bobbed gently between sleep and waking, like when he would drift off during long car rides and his father carried him—still dozing—from the back seat of the car and up to his room.

It was quiet around him, a deeper silence than any he'd ever experienced before swaddling him like a thick blanket. Although, perhaps silence wasn't the best word for it. There were things like sounds, but they weren't sounds, not exactly. They didn't hit his ears, but somewhere else instead. Behind his eyes maybe, though they were closed.

He tried to raise his head but found it to be too heavy with exhaustion, and so instead, he buried it even deeper into the softness of the ground. It felt like grass, and he wondered vaguely if he was outside somewhere and if The Oldest was with him, before falling back into dreaming.

In his dreams, the grass on the ground beneath him wasn't grass at all, but long pale mushroom stalks. No, not that either. It was fingers. Thousands of them, cradling his face like a pillow, stroking his cheeks like his mother did when he was sad or lonely.

He was still drowsy, even inside the dream, and as he nestled deeper into the thousand fingers, they nestled deeper into him, pushing gently into his mouth, his nostrils, his ears. Digging their way into his eyes. It wasn't a bad feeling. Just strange. He hadn't really understood before, he mused vaguely, how small he was in comparison to his body. There was so much space inside of him. So much empty space. Filling up.

*

After all the confusion in the woods, we decided the smartest thing to do was simply to return to The Lake House for dinner. If anything was really wrong, we could have The Adults sort it out.

The sun was low in the sky and the air around us grew progressively darker as we made our way out of the forest. The Twins now led our procession, walking with enough confidence that only one or two of the rest of us harbored any doubt that we'd make it out of the woods before nightfall. The rest of us followed behind, all except for The Baby and The One with the Beautiful Voice who—we were now certain—were already back at The House.

There was a disgruntled feeling permeating the group, all of us dwelling on our own small worries and hurts. One of us felt rebuffed by another. One was worried that none of The Adults had called us for dinner. One wished that we didn't have to leave the forest. One was trying to remember something that kept slipping away. One was twisting their thoughts into strange loops wrapping tighter and tighter around each other. One wanted to go home. One was somewhere else already.

The forest, which had been so thick and vast on our way in, seemed to shrink as we exited, spitting us out onto the flooded lawn of The Lake House after what seemed like no more than ten minutes of walking. All the windows in The House were dark except a single illuminated pane in The Children's Wing.

We turned to each other.

Did they go out to eat? we asked.

Did they leave us behind?

Did The Others go with them?

The Boy Twin, who was tired and hungry, kicked at the ground so hard that a sheet of water splashed out over the grass.

What the hell?! he screamed.

The rest of us walked around him toward The Children's

Wing. Eventually, he joined us, running a little to catch up. The illuminated window was on the third floor, and so we climbed up the stone staircase, leaving damp footprints behind us as we went. The House was quiet, still, almost as if lost in thought. There was a funny smell in the air—musky, like damp clothes left sitting too long in the washing machine.

Hello?! we called.

We're back!

Is anyone home?

Where is everyone?

No one called back to us. Not even The House itself creaked in response.

When we finally reached the third floor, a few of us hung back in the stairwell.

You go ahead, we urged The Twins, who had once again charged ahead of us.

You go ahead, and we'll wait here.

The Boy Twin snorted and rolled his eyes conspiratorially at The Girl Twin. She smiled back tersely and opened the door.

The third floor of The Children's Wing wasn't a floor so much as one large room. Though Our Grandfather claimed he used to throw parties there, it now served as a sort of storage area. It had no furniture of its own, but was crammed full of unused pieces belonging to other rooms—wrap-around leather couches covered in plastic, incomplete barstool sets, a bar cart in the corner covered in dusty bottles, shelves pushed together into the center of the room, a mysterious collection of birdcages, gilded mirrors with cracked faces draped in gauze . . . Besides all the furniture, there were some boxes stuffed in the corner, several rolled-up rugs, and an ancient, half-rotting grand piano. Our Young Aunt sat there now, perched on the bench with her back against the peeling wallpaper and The Baby in her lap. Her fingers lightly rested on the keys, which made no sound.

Is anyone in there? we called from the hallway.

The Girl Twin was about to answer when Our Young Aunt began speaking.

"There you are!" she cried, as if she had been looking for us all day. "I've been calling for you. We all have. It's time for dinner and no one knew where you all had gone off to. I was beginning to get worried."

Where is everyone? asked The Boy Twin.

"They're all in The Main House," she replied, picking up something from her lap that The Baby had dropped and feeding it back to her. "They've been waiting for you. It's time for dinner."

But none of the lights were on, said The Liar, who had come into the room behind The Twins. *No one was there. We looked.*

Our Young Aunt hummed absently in response while The Baby munched on something clasped in her chubby little fist.

"It's time for dinner," she repeated as if she hadn't heard.

"I've been waiting up for you here, but The Baby's hungry. We should go to The Main House."

The Baby leaned over Our Young Aunt's shoulder, her arm extended toward the browning strips of old wallpaper. Behind them, the crumbling plaster was dotted all over with fuzzy black spots of mold and decay. The Baby grabbed a chalky handful and shoved it cheerfully into her mouth. Bits of white powder puffed from her lips as she chewed. Our Young Aunt patted her absently on her back.

"Good girl," she murmured, and then turning back to the rest of us, "let's go to the house. Everyone's waiting for you there."

She stood, allowing The Baby to tear one last strip of paper from the wall, and then walked past us into the stairwell. Seeing no other option available to us, we followed.

*

The Liar and The One Who Runs Away hung back from the rest of us and, as we neared the hallway connecting The Children's Wing to the rest of The Lake House, The One Who Runs Away pulled at the elbow of his younger cousin's shirt and whispered to her.

I have something to show you. Let them go ahead—we can catch up to them later.

The two stopped and let the rest of us enter through the second-floor library before retracing our steps back into The Children's Wing. The Liar did not know The One Who Runs

Away well—none of us did—but she cautiously followed as he led her into the little yellow kitchen.

Once there, he pulled a little glass bottle half-full of amber liquid from the cupboard, along with a folded-up picnic blanket studded with little blue tassels. The Liar was suddenly overcome with an old memory from infanthood of Our Late Grandmother laying her down upon the blanket in a field of clover. Though she could only recall snippets of the moment—a pair of breadcrumbs trapped in the corner of Our Late Grandmother's mouth, a fly buzzing by her ear, a green smear where the clover had crushed against the fabric—she could remember the exact sensation of the blades of grass pushing up through the fibers of the blanket and nudging against her infant fist.

It's outside, her cousin said, his back to her. *Where we snuck off to last night when you thought we were keeping you up. I thought you'd want to see.*

The mention of the events of the previous night set The Liar on edge. Though she had no way of arguing against her cousins' version of things, she was still convinced they were all lying to her. It hadn't been The Baby causing all that ruckus, she was sure of it. The Baby could talk, but only barely. Just simple phrases she parroted or requests to be picked up or given food. The voices The Liar heard had been coming from outside. And they spoke in full sentences. They called her name.

We're already late for dinner, she said, heading back toward The Others. *Maybe we should go another time.*

The One Who Runs Away looked back at her and, for a moment, there was something thorny and desperately sad in his expression that The Liar recognized and yet struggled to understand. Out of all of the cousins, he—in some ways— felt nearest to her. Both were on the outside of things in one way or another. But he was also much older and had a life and an inner world he kept separate, not just from her, but from all of us. She felt unsure of what to say, how to act.

It'll only take a moment, he said.

*

We climbed back down the spiral staircase and out into the night, the damp yard soaking through our shoes and chilling our feet. Though The Liar was afraid we'd return to the forest, The One Who Runs Away turned instead to walk to the front yard, stopping in the center, where a raised part of the ground was spared from the damp. He unfurled the picnic blanket and sat down on it, gesturing for The Liar to do the same. As she did so, she noticed that white mushrooms ringed the ground around us and was careful not to step on any.

Try this, The One Who Runs Away said, holding out the bottle to her.

The Liar started.

I'm not supposed to have that, she said, *and neither are you.*
It's not what you think it is, he said. *Trust me.*

And though she didn't, she took a sip anyway, just a small one, expecting the same strange burning sensation she had experienced when she accidentally took a swig of her father's bourbon once. Instead, though, she tasted a different flavor, one so far off from what she had been expecting that she couldn't put a name to it at first.

She passed the bottle under a beam of moonlight to confirm that it did indeed look how she remembered it and then took another sip.

Strange, right? said The One Who Runs Away as he fiddled with the tassels on the blanket.

Why does it taste like . . . milk? asked The Liar, though she couldn't see how there could be any reasonable explanation. It didn't even taste like milk exactly, more like heavy cream and something else, too, something she didn't really have a name for but that made her picture crystalline dew dripping off of flower petals, but that sounded too odd to say aloud.

I don't know, said her cousin, *but isn't that weird? It doesn't taste like that inside. It tastes normal. I tried it. But it tasted like that when we went out last night.*

The Liar took another swig, trying to position the bottle so the liquid caught the moonlight as it trickled into her mouth. It didn't change color but it tasted the same. She began to get a warm, buzzy feeling in her chest. She wanted to lie down.

Why don't you lie down? asked The One Who Runs Away. *We can watch the stars like we did last night.*

She did and he lay down next to her. When she looked up at the sky, it seemed more crowded than usual. Behind every star seemed to hide another star. If she bent her neck from side to side, she could see around them, but even the stars behind the stars had more stars behind them. Dizzying.

Do you want to know what happened last night? her cousin asked.

Someone else seemed to lie down on her other side, but when The Liar looked, no one was there. She turned toward The One Who Runs Away, who didn't look back at her, but instead down at his hands, which he was using to carefully unpick one of the blue tassels before tying it back together in a funny series of loops.

Yes, she said. *Tell me.*

*

We snuck out pretty soon after the rest of you went to bed. Though, I guess you were still up. I didn't know. Anyways, we came out here, to this spot. I remember it because of the mushrooms. See how they're growing? It's cool—I've never seen mushrooms grow like that before. There're three circles, see? The one around us and then these two here touching it. It's like a triangle.

The Liar looked at where her cousin was pointing. She saw the ring surrounding them and then the empty ring in front of her and the one right next to it, which wasn't empty. There was someone lying inside, covered in clover and flowers. She blinked. No, it wasn't a person at all, but a mound of dirt. She didn't know why she'd thought it was a person. Maybe it was because of how the mushrooms around it were moving. No, not moving. That couldn't be it. It was how they were flickering in the moonlight. She took another sip of the liquid and felt it coat her throat. It was like drinking butter and clover honey. She was tired. She lay back and closed her eyes while her cousin continued.

We were just drinking and talking and watching the stars. We thought the drink thing was weird, how it tasted different, but that was what was fun about it. The stars were so bright. There was one . . . at first, we thought it was a planet, like Venus or something. It was brighter than the others. And the light was different—reddish almost, but still glowing white. It started getting bigger and bigger, almost like it was coming towards us, but then we realized that it wasn't moving; it was sucking the rest of them in.

The rest of what in? asked The Liar.

The rest of the stars. It was eating them. It kept eating and eating until they were all gone, until it was the only one left.

The Liar looked up at the sky. Right above her was a bright star, larger than the others, shining with a strange rusty light.

It was completely dark when we heard the noise. You know how you said you heard something last night? So did I. I'm sorry I lied to you this morning. I just didn't think anyone else would understand. It sounded like a baby crying, or like a little kid laughing. I couldn't tell what it was, but it was coming from the woods.

What about The Others? asked The Liar.

The One Who Runs Away looked confused for a moment and then his expression cleared.

Oh, I don't know if they heard. I think they had already gone down to the lake by then maybe.

The lake? You guys walked all the way there?

Yeah, it's not that far. That's what I wanted to show you.

Why did you sneak out anyway? It's not like we don't have free time during the day.

I thought you, out of anyone, would understand.

The Liar did understand, even though she didn't feel like saying it right then. The two didn't tend to be included in Family things the way the rest of us were. For different reasons, of course, which—to The Liar—made all the difference. Because, while The One Who Runs Away's place within The Family had everything to do with his parents and nothing, really, to do with him at all, it was The Liar herself who most of The Adults found confusing at best (and she didn't like to dwell on what they thought of her at worst.)

Though she knew that The One Who Runs Away's parents caused him great pain in many ways, she was sometimes jealous of how they didn't seem to care what anyone thought of them. Her father didn't either, or at least he said he didn't, but he wasn't going to put himself out on her account. And, though her mother was pained when people called The Liar the wrong name or said she was an attention seeker or put her with the boys, she wasn't going to either. She didn't like conflict or people thinking badly about her. She would tell The Liar later how wrong it had been and how she had felt hurt by it on The Liar's behalf, but in the moment, she rarely said anything.

The Liar once overheard her mother talking about her. Her mother was on her computer, shut up in the little room—no bigger than a closet—that The Liar's parents used as an office, but the summer humidity made the door swell so that it didn't fit into the frame the right way and The Liar could see through the crack. From her crouched position in the hallway, The Liar had no way of knowing who it was her mother was speaking to, but the way her mother relayed the story of The Liar's life as if it was something that belonged to her made The Liar sure that this person was someone she didn't know. The only way to listen without getting her feelings hurt was to pretend she was someone else. As her mother told the computer how grateful she was to the person on the other side because "no one else understands how hard it is, how strong you have to be every day to bear it," The Liar tried to picture the child her mother described. The Liar herself wasn't anywhere at all.

I guess you probably just wanted to feel what it was like to be out there on your own. To explore.

The One Who Runs Away hummed in vague agreement.

What'd you see there? At the lake.

We can't explain it. We have to show you.

The voice didn't belong to The One Who Runs Away.

The Liar whipped her head around to find The Oldest lying next to her in the grass. She hadn't remembered him coming out with us, but perhaps he followed behind and she just hadn't realized. Her head felt funny and she wanted to sleep.

You seem tired, The Oldest said, in a voice that sounded like he was talking to a much younger child. *Why don't you hop on my back? I'll take you. We can all go together.*

I'm hungry, The Liar complained. *I want to go in for dinner.*

The Liar looked back up at the sky. There were fewer stars than she remembered there being before. The red light seemed to pulse like a beating heart. She felt a hand in hers, but when she looked down, it had been pulled away, leaving behind only a knot of strings pulled from the picnic blanket and fashioned into a kind of bracelet. She didn't know whether or not to feel touched by this gesture.

Let her go, The One Who Runs Away said. *We can go another time. I don't want to be late for dinner.*

You're sure? The Oldest asked.

She felt him watching her, but it must have been out of the corner of his eye because his face was turned away from her. He was looking instead at the mound inside of the third circle. He reached his hand out to touch it gently, stroking it like a cheek. She walked over to see. At the top of the mound, something white and smooth was poking out of the grass and vines. She peered closer. It opened its eyes and looked at her for a second before sinking deeper into the ground.

She dropped to her knees and pawed at it, but it was only dirt and grass now.

Was that . . . ? she asked.

Just leave it, replied The One Who Runs Away. *It's nothing. Let's go in before they start without us.*

She rubbed her eyes and, after a moment's hesitation, slipped her hand through the knotted bracelet. When she looked up, she saw The Oldest loping into the woods. His gait was strange, oddly strangled. But before she could determine why that was, he stepped into the shadows and disappeared.

Where is he off to? she asked.

No reply came.

*

The rest of us filed into the big kitchen behind Our Young Aunt. The Baby was in The Boy Twin's arms now, wriggling and babbling as she shoved fistfuls of drywall into her sticky mouth. He didn't know how she got there, though as soon as he wondered this, a vague memory appeared of his sister handing her to him before going up to talk to Our Young Aunt. He wasn't experienced with young children and struggled to balance her on his hip. As he shifted her around, she looked up at him and cooed, reaching her hands out to his face. He stuck his tongue out at her and she smiled. She had so many teeth coming in. Little sharp ones all over her mouth, crowding each other out.

The Adults were huddled around the dinner table, eerily silent. They didn't turn to greet us when we entered. Instead, they focused on eating. The dinner table was almost overflowing with food: fruits—even the kinds we rarely ate, figs and melons and pomegranates—platters of vegetables smothered in butter and garlic, scalloped potatoes, and rolls steaming from the oven, whole carcasses of all kinds leaking bloody liquid.

We approached the table and tried to find places to sit, but there seemed to be more Adults than usual, though there wasn't anyone there we didn't recognize. Some of us tried to squeeze into seats only to find that the chairs we thought were empty were already occupied. Some of us found spots next to our parents, but when we looked up at them, we found that they were not our parents, but someone else entirely—someone we could recognize as Family but whose name we couldn't quite place.

The Crybaby tried to slip in next to her mother. There were no free seats, so she just stood behind her mother's elbow, waiting for her to notice. When she didn't, The Crybaby tugged at her shirt sleeve. Something opened in the back of her mother's head and growled at her, a deep thrumming sound like the warning cry of a large bird. She began to cry and backed into The Adult in the other seat next to her. They picked her up and, when she looked at them, she saw that their head was turned away from her, though she didn't know how that was possible. She closed her eyes and felt the person holding her pat her on the shoulder and then nudge her lips open with a fork. After only a moment of resistance, she chewed on what they fed her. It tasted like some sort of meat. Ground beef but fresher.

"Do you like it, honey? Doesn't it taste good?"

The person holding her spoke in her mother's voice, but she didn't dare open her eyes to look.

*

The Liar watched us through the window from outside. Her socks were soaked through and she was hungry. She wanted to come in. But the scene on the other side of the window made her pause.

The Adults were all sitting strangely. Some were turned around, seemingly resting their chins on the backs of their chairs with their backs turned to the table. They were utterly motionless. None of them looked at the table, and she couldn't see any of their faces, even those who were facing the window, seemingly staring right at it. Everyone else, The Liar saw, was crowded around the table, shoving food into their mouths. None of them met her eyes, and their own eyes had a strange glazed look to them. Where they pressed their bodies against the edge of the table, dark splotches appeared on their shirts.

All around, there was movement, but The Liar couldn't figure out who was moving. Everyone seemed to be staying still besides the frantic motion of their hands carrying food to their mouths.

She kicked her feet in the grass and weighed her options. She could go in to dinner despite the strangeness of the scene in front of her, or she could go up to bed, alone and hungry. Her third option, which she knew she wouldn't want to take, would be to follow The Oldest down through the woods to the lake.

She looked up and, without meaning to, met Our Grandfather's eyes. He was sitting in the middle of the rest of us, the only one not eating. She raised her hand tentatively to wave at him, but he didn't wave back. He was gazing, she realized, not at her, but at The One Who Runs Away, who stood right behind her. Our Grandfather's face was difficult to read, which she had always found to be the case. Something in his expression reminded her of when she had seen him at The Twins' house for Christmas last year. It was then that she first heard about the houses neighboring The Lake House, the seemingly unstoppable mold they were all plagued by, the vines that relentlessly tore at the outside walls, the way they sunk deeper and deeper into the soil each month. Their old owners had to sell, which Our Grandfather saw as an opportunity for The Family. After all, he'd told the dinner table as everyone laughed and jockeyed for his attention, his house was the only one spared, so he clearly knew what he was doing.

As he spoke that night, Our Grandfather looked proud but weary, too, already absorbed by the work that was to come. It was the same way now, and this expression passed from his face, through the kitchen window, and into The One Who Runs Away's indistinct features.

Should we join them? The One Who Runs Away asked.

We went inside.

*

Inside, it was all just fine. Or, at least, that's how it looked to The Liar at first. The Adults were sitting normally at the table, doing adult things—cutting up their food with knives and forks, spilling a little wine on the table as they topped up their glasses, lowering their voices at points in the conversation when they wanted to speak to each other without us overhearing.

She looked around the room, locating the rest of us in turn. The Baby was being held by one of The Adults, though The Liar didn't quite recognize who it was . . . A distant aunt, perhaps, or one of the old cousins. The Twins and The Secret Keeper sat at the far side of the table, chatting to each other in low tones. The One with the Beautiful Voice was sitting with The Oldest, who had somehow beaten her to the table. The two seemed to be chatting to each other as well, though whenever The Liar looked at them, their mouths didn't seem to be moving. The Crybaby sat on The Oldest's lap, which seemed odd to The Liar. She had never really noticed The Oldest interacting with the younger cousins before. The Crybaby ate with her eyes closed.

So, that's it, The Liar thought. Everyone was within view. Except somewhere in the back of her mind, she felt the niggling sensation that the person she had been looking for (a mound of earth, a pale face within) wasn't there. She counted, just to make sure. Eight young faces. Nine if she included herself. Everyone accounted for.

The One Who Runs Away had pulled up a seat at the table next to Our Grandfather and was in rapt conversation with the old man. Our Grandfather, The Liar noticed, still wasn't eating. The plate in front of him was empty. Instead, he took long sips from a stout glass full of amber liquid. Somehow, The Liar was sure that, if she were to take a sip of this drink, it would sting like her father's bourbon. When The One Who Runs Away noticed The Liar looking at him, he waved her over. After a moment's hesitation, she joined.

The Liar tentatively approached Our Grandfather and sat herself down next to him. She saw how The One Who Runs Away looked eagerly between her and Our Grandfather like he was trying to build something between them. Nothing emerged. Our Grandfather looked at her, grimaced, and then stared down at his empty plate. The conversation he had been having with The One Who Runs Away, about navigating town halls and zoning laws, died, as did the smile on The One Who Runs Away's face. The Liar felt bad for him then, without really understanding why.

A plate that seemed to belong to The Crybaby, who sat next to The Liar on The Oldest's lap, was set in front of

The Liar's chair, piled high with untouched food. The Liar, aware of disappointing both Our Grandfather and The One Who Runs Away in different ways, decided the only thing for her to do was to eat. Steam rose from the rolls and buttered vegetables. It smelled incredible.

Are you eating this? she asked The Crybaby.

The Crybaby, hearing The Liar's voice, finally opened her eyes. She looked over at her cousin, who was gesturing toward the full plate of food in front of her. She shook her head and The Liar started to eat. Tentatively, The Crybaby looked past The Liar, where she found Our Grandfather watching the rest of us eating. She smiled at him and he smiled back, which surprised her. From all of her interactions with him, she had always been under the impression that he didn't really care for any of us. He didn't really seem to like children much.

Cheered by this, she looked up at the person whose lap she was sitting on. Though she was expecting to see her mother, she did not feel shocked when she saw that it was— in fact—The Oldest. That must have been what accounted for her confusion earlier. His long brown hair always pushed into his face . . . Focused on his food, he didn't seem to notice her. Now that she was feeling better, she took in the dinner spread in front of her. Everything looked warm and delicious. Her stomach growled. She leaned over toward The Liar.

Could you pass the sweet potatoes?

As she spooned two potatoes onto her plate and slathered them with butter, her eyes passed over the seat across from her. Our Late Grandmother's place. She started. How did she end up in the same seat again, across from the same horrible chair? She looked down quickly, focusing on her plate, on the rhythmic tapping of The One Who Runs Away's foot on the ground.

Someone was sitting in the chair. She saw it. Just briefly, just out of the corner of her eye, but someone was there. She wanted to see, to verify that it was just a normal person and not some kind of ghost or monster. But she also didn't want to see. She felt stuck. She wanted to cry, but she was tired of everyone making fun of her, so she decided she would try to be brave instead. She would check. But she didn't want to look it in the face, because what if it was Our Late Grandmother's face? And what if it wasn't a face at all but a grinning skull? Or something in between the two? That, she thought, would be the worst possible thing.

So instead she began slipping down low, inching off The Oldest's lap and under the table.

When her feet finally touched the old, patterned carpet, she crouched and scurried underneath the checkered table-cloth. Beneath the table, it was quiet and strange. Legs kicked and feet tapped the floor and there was plenty of movement and sound, but it all seemed oddly muffled, like being underwater. There were so many legs in comparison to people, so many that The Crybaby felt as though she were losing count. Some of the legs were wrapped in pants or skirts or leggings, and some only shorts; some feet were covered by shoes or sandals, some had socks, and some had nothing on them at all. She couldn't place who each pair belonged to. They swayed and bumped and pressed the floor like separate creatures entirely.

The feet across from her did not do anything the rest of the feet were doing. They were bare, placed on the floor a shoulder's length apart from each other, and entirely still. See? she thought to herself. There's nothing wrong with them. They're just normal feet.

But they weren't normal feet. Something *was* wrong with them. She couldn't quite put her finger on it, but the shape of them wasn't right. She inched closer, straining to see. When she was about halfway across the table, it hit her. They were normal feet, but they were turned around backwards.

At first, she thought that the person sitting had just turned around in their seat, but that wasn't it, because the knees were pointing forward like they were supposed to. It was the feet themselves that were backwards, the toes pointing back at the chair behind them. As she realized this, a groan of *no, no, no* rising in her chest, she saw the torso shift a little and then a hand appeared at the tablecloth, pulling it up to make way for a head being slowly lowered down to look at her. It was dark, shadowed, but she could recognize the face, the familiar smile, though the teeth glinting out at her were not where they were supposed to be.

*

The Liar startled as she heard something that sounded like a cry from under the table. No one else seemed to have noticed and, when she bent down to check under the tablecloth, she found nothing there. Maybe it wasn't a cry, she thought. Things in The Lake House had a funny, shifting quality to them. More and more often, The Liar found her own senses to be wrong somehow. Or at least her first interpretation of them. As she thought this, the taste of the food in her mouth changed. She had been enjoying some sort of potato salad that had bacon in it and a mustard dressing. Only moments before, it had been rich and creamy on her tongue. But now it turned to something quite different, something thick and mineral and sharp.

Can I be excused? she asked.

No one responded to her, so she left the table and began walking back toward The Children's Wing, The Twins and The Secret Keeper following close behind her.

*

People were moving around her. The Crybaby could sense this, could see out of the corners of her eyes that the legs around her were darting this way and that in shimmers like schools of fish, but she was eating some sort of fruit she'd never had before—a melon with golden skin and golden flesh and a flavor that was close to marmalade. It was fascinating. She looked closely at the rind, tracking a tiny white vein up through the body. She imagined sunlight pumping through the vein like blood.

She was sitting in the floor. No, on the floor. Or maybe underneath it, she couldn't tell. If she was underneath it, she was still right side up somehow, like gravity had reversed itself on her. She wiggled her toes and felt the damp soil between them. She bit down on the place the vein ran through the flesh of the melon and, after swallowing, finally looked up at the feet beneath the table. The feet, the ones that had scared her before, were gone. Most were, it seemed.

She brushed the dirt off her knees and climbed up, out into the room. Though food was still out, the table had been tidied up—dirty plates and silverware cleared, napkins brushed off and refolded. She hadn't noticed it happening and—though she knew she should feel guilty about it—she was pleased she didn't have to help.

For some reason, it took her a moment to register the presence of The One with the Beautiful Voice, who sat with The Baby perched on his lap. Everyone else was gone, and he sat so quietly and so still that he didn't even seem like a person at first. More like something growing up from the soil below. No, not the soil, she was inside. The floorboards, maybe. It was almost funny to see such a small child holding an even smaller one, but there was also a serious manner about him that made the scene seem natural. The One with the Beautiful Voice looked up at The Crybaby and smiled.

I'm going to go watch the stars. They're so beautiful out here, so bright. Do you want to join me?

Somewhere, far in the back of The Crybaby's head, a

voice protested. Something was wrong. The way The One with the Beautiful Voice spoke didn't sound like him but like a version of him that had grown up many years into the future. And where was everyone else? But the rest of her squashed these thoughts: it seemed so nice, didn't it, to go outside? The warm breeze and cool grass and the open night sky.

Don't worry, said a small voice at her side. *The Others will join us soon.*

She was walking through the corridors of The Children's Wing. She wasn't sure how we had gotten there. She didn't remember leaving the dinner table. The Baby was balanced on her hip, her fingers snagged in The Crybaby's hair, pulling and untangling, the little fingers working out every knot and snarl. The One with the Beautiful Voice walked alongside her, holding her free hand. Beneath her fingers, her cousin's hand felt hot and strangely hollow. She felt a sudden urge to look at her cousin's face, but something deep in her brain stem warned her not to. That if she were to look at The One with the Beautiful Voice, she would not see her cousin at all, but an animal of some kind, wearing her cousin's skin.

They continued on. Through the stairwell and out the door to the spot The Liar had claimed The Others were the night before, the raised section of yard, the three mushroom circles all touching. She lay down on the grass and closed her eyes. On the ground to her right, she felt a small body settle down next to her and then the smaller body of The

Baby wriggling over her chest. She opened her eyes and saw that her sister wasn't there. It had been a trick of sensation, the strong night breeze blowing over her body. The Baby was somewhere off closer to the trees, crawling through the brush. She couldn't see her well, just the grass and bushes bobbing and bending as she passed through, the occasional flash of heel or hand.

She turned to her cousin sitting next to her. Though they were friendly with each other at Family events, being around the same age, The Crybaby didn't actually know very much about The One with the Beautiful Voice other than the pretend games they both liked to play together and what she had overheard The Adults saying about him in passing. She felt too tired to play a game and tried to think of something to say to him instead. She felt embarrassed, never totally comfortable talking to other people unless she was playing make-believe.

You sing, right? That's what my mom said. She said you're really good at it.

The One with the Beautiful Voice nodded.

What made you start? How did you know you could do it?

The One with the Beautiful Voice was quiet, seemingly lost in thought. After a long moment, during which The Crybaby began to assume he didn't want to answer, he finally spoke.

It's hard to explain in words, he said. *Do you want me to show you?*

Without knowing exactly why she was doing so, The Crybaby nodded. The One with the Beautiful Voice turned to her, and The Crybaby noticed that there was something different about his eyes, like they were turned around to be facing inside out or upside down. She couldn't quite put her finger on it because they were almost identical to his normal eyes, but something was different. They seemed to blink from the bottom instead of the top.

Shall I sing for you? her cousin asked.

She wasn't really interested in hearing her cousin sing. But she wanted to be polite. And anyways, it would be so nice to lie back in the grass, she thought, to let the music wash over her. She nodded again.

The One with the Beautiful Voice opened his mouth wide and then opened it further, not out but back, a tunnel widening in his throat. There was something inside of it, nestled past the root of his tongue. Or where the root of his tongue might have been. The Crybaby drew closer, trying to get a good look at it, but all she could see were the twigs and soil and dead leaves stuffing his mouth. As the singing started—a shrill cacophony of screaming insects so loud that it invaded every one of her senses, filling her up until there was no space for anything else left inside of her—it opened its eyes and looked back.

*

The Twins worked together to move the crib out of The Girl Twin and The Secret Keeper's bedroom. There wasn't any particular reason to do so. But something about the crib's presence made it feel as though The Baby might appear within it at any moment.

With the crib moved out into the hallway, we shut and locked the door, pushing a bookshelf in front of it for good measure. Four of us were holing up in there together—safety in numbers. It was a faint safety, but it was the best we had available to us.

The Girl Twin moved her things over to The Secret Keeper's bed, allowing The Boy Twin and The Liar to take over the one she had been sleeping in. If she had been able to choose, The Girl Twin would have rather stayed with her brother. When she spent longer than a few days with The Secret Keeper, she started to tire of trying to keep up. She liked a certain amount of order and certainty, but she liked to let herself be a part of things too. When she played with her brother or The Liar or her friends at home, she didn't think much about what she was supposed to be doing or how it might look to an outside observer. Being with The Secret Keeper made her feel mature and a little superior, but it also reminded her a bit of how she felt when she was at home with her mother. Like she was trying her best to be a grown-up but didn't quite know how.

But it wouldn't be right to make The Secret Keeper share with The Liar. The Adults wouldn't have allowed it, and The Secret Keeper agreed with The Adults about most things.

The Secret Keeper came in late from dinner, though the rest of us had been sure she was following right behind. When we opened the door to her knock, she seemed distracted and didn't look any of us in the eye. Instead, she had gone straight to the bathroom to scrub the dirt off of her hands. The Girl Twin felt a little relieved but also abandoned, left to figure out what to do on her own while The Secret Keeper attended to her own private thoughts. The Liar, too, was acting in ways The Girl Twin hadn't expected. Like the rest of us, she seemed anxious and confused, but there was an air of sadness about her, too, that The Girl Twin couldn't quite place. Maybe, The Girl Twin considered, it was sadness stemming from the lost promise of the trip, a sadness The Girl Twin shared. This made her feel close to her cousin, and she tried to think of a way to express this to The Liar, who stood near the window now, looking out over the backyard. The Girl Twin sidled up to her.

What're you looking at? she asked. She had meant to say something reassuring, something about how they'd have time to play outside together tomorrow, but the words didn't come naturally.

The Liar pointed down to the flooded backyard, where thousands of stars shone up at us through the grass. She turned to face The Girl Twin, her expression inscrutable.

Did they tell you about last night? she asked.

The Girl Twin didn't know what she was talking about. And who was "they"?

She was there too, you know, The Liar said, pointing to The Secret Keeper. *She didn't tell you?*

The Girl Twin looked over at The Secret Keeper, who sat huddled on their now-shared bed, hugging her knees to her chest like she was trying to keep herself together. The Girl Twin knew that The Liar was probably telling the truth, but she didn't want it to be the truth because it would mean that The Secret Keeper was lying to her among other, even less thinkable implications.

The water's higher than it was yesterday, murmured The Liar. *Like a moat.*

A breeze passed over the river and through the yard, causing the reflected stars to tremble in their pools.

When we stayed behind for a bit while the rest of you went to dinner, he pointed something out to me, The Liar continued. *I don't think I would have noticed it on my own but now I can't stop thinking about it.*

She pointed up at the sky and The Girl Twin followed her finger. The moon hung lonely there, half-hidden behind a cloud. Around it, the sky was strangely empty, only a small smattering of stars blinking out from the black. As she continued looking, she noticed one of them shining brighter than the rest, a bright reddish-gold glow like a planet. Mars maybe. But it was not Mars. She knew nothing of astronomy, but she was sure of this. It glowed brighter the longer she looked at it, and the stars surrounding it seemed to flicker out at the corners of her vision.

It's beautiful, the Girl Twin breathed, not knowing what else to say.

The floor creaked as The Secret Keeper walked over to join us. She put her chin on The Girl Twin's shoulder, the point of it digging uncomfortably into her skin.

Look here, said The Liar, now pointing down at the flooded lawn.

It took The Girl Twin a second to realize what The Liar was pointing out, but then it came upon her all at once, and she didn't know how she could have missed it before. Unlike the real sky above her, the reflected sky was overflowing with stars, little beams of light packed so closely together that they seemed almost to bump into each other as the surface of the water wavered under the breeze.

The Girl Twin looked back up at the real sky and found it nearly empty.

That's someone else's sky, said The Secret Keeper from behind us, a slight wobble in her voice. *It's not for us.*

The Girl Twin turned around to look at her cousin, whose face was white and drawn.

What do you mean? she asked.

I don't know how to explain it. Anything I say seems crazy. I feel crazy. I don't feel like I understand anything that's going on here. Or like I know anyone. Everyone seems like a stranger to me.

Even me? The Girl Twin asked.

I don't know, said The Secret Keeper. *You don't seem like a stranger right now, but if I turn around and then look back at you, I don't know if you'll stay the same.*

The Girl Twin nodded. She knew what her cousin meant. Things seemed to change here in ways she didn't know how to get a grasp on. She knew she should be scared, and she was, or at least she was intellectually. The feeling was just a little bit removed from an actual sensation, though, and was difficult to access. She had gotten her period only a year or so prior and it reminded her of how it felt when she took Tylenol to soothe her cramps. The painkiller didn't quite make the cramps go away; they were still there, only blanketed, removed from her body by a few degrees.

The Lake House seemed to operate by a different logic than the way things worked in her home or at school or even at the houses of her friends and family. And though she didn't trust this logic, she had gotten used to it, had grown accustomed to the difference. She could see that The Others had too. Not The Secret Keeper it seemed, but the rest of us certainly, each in our own way. It was important, The Girl Twin thought, to adapt to your surroundings. That's something else her father always said. She stared hard at the reflected sky before turning away and getting ready for bed.

*

The Liar couldn't sleep. She didn't know what time it was, but she knew it must have been late. It was already too late when they had dinner, she thought, much later than it should have been. She lay very still and quiet on her back, The Boy Twin snoring lightly in her ear. He had fallen asleep right away, despite his promises that he would be "on the lookout for danger." The Girl Twin had gone next; The Liar heard her breathing start to deepen and slow an hour or so ago. The Secret Keeper was still awake. The Liar could hear her tossing and turning in bed, occasionally pausing to get out and examine the night sky or to mutter something quietly to herself.

There were other noises, too, shuffling sounds along the floor, like small animals moving there. At one point, she thought she felt something try to crawl onto the bed near her feet. She had kicked, hard, and her foot collided with something, but it wasn't like a body, more like a gust of hot, dry air. Something light and thin tore off against her toes and stuck there, but she didn't want to see what it was.

There was whispering, too, the sound of a conversation, the right tones for human speech. It was loud enough that she should have been able to pick out at least the occasional phrase, but she couldn't find even a single word she recognized. Though it sounded like a dialogue, it could have been a single person talking ceaselessly, and she couldn't determine if it was coming from The Secret Keeper or from somewhere else.

As she listened, she thought of her "real life" home, the loneliness of the apartment when she came home from school, the way the sounds outside (conversations between friends, laughter, barking dogs, the sounds of cars and buses and motorcycles) seemed to blow through the empty rooms like ghosts. The loneliness of schooldays: being kept in for recess to complete work she didn't know how to do, the warring pity and contempt in the eyes of the adults there, being grouped together with children she had nothing in common with, the incredible difficulty of paying attention to lessons or talking to her peers, the surprise and confusion she felt whenever her teacher called on her, the isolation of the nurse's bathroom. The loneliness of the dinner table: her father on his phone, resentment radiating off of him in waves, and her mother trying hard to make conversation, asking her the same questions every day, as if this time the answers might be the ones she wanted them to be.

And she thought, too, of The Lake House and her time here and how she wished the weekend wasn't coming to an end soon. Even with the strangeness of it all. There was something about being here that made her feel different, like the way things always were had tugged and torn against the sharp treetops, leaving space for something new. Leaving space for her, maybe. Everything around her seemed to be in a state of change—the living things dying; the dead things growing new life; soil turning over; the short, jewel-like life cycles of insects and flowers and small animals spinning and spinning, each facet glinting to her in turn. She felt like a part of things here. She wanted us to be a part of it with her, to stay with her.

It would be better if The Adults were the ones slipping away. If they would just go, she thought, then maybe it wouldn't all feel so scary. If they returned to their normal lives, we could stay here forever, could be with each other so easily without them. There was so much to explore, so much to do. We could eat outside every night. We could wear whatever we wanted or nothing at all, and we could grow our hair out so long that it skimmed the grass when we walked. We could run and scream and laugh when we were happy and cry when we were sad and sleep together in a big pile like puppies. We could claw into the dirt and dig, deeper and deeper, clay and rot and living things squishing between our fingers and then: not even *between* but *into*, the dirt grabbing hold of us and squeezing back.

As she thought this, one of the things dragging across the floor managed to make it up onto the foot of the bed. She should have been scared, but she wasn't. Just curious. She waited to see what it would do. She thought it might crawl up to her, but instead, it settled down on top of the blankets, the heat of its body soaking down until it reached her feet. She adjusted a little, to make space and to be more comfortable, and then finally fell into a deep sleep.

*

Her sisters. Where were her sisters?

The Secret Keeper awoke with a jolt. Somehow, she had fallen asleep without realizing it. She had been in her bed, The Girl Twin tossing and turning beside her, and then, suddenly, she was awake, staring at the blank black of the ceiling at night, listening to the snores and murmurs of her cousins around her.

But where were her sisters?

She was supposed to look after them. It was important to her mother. It was important to her, too, in a different sort of way. She had done a good job of it so far, hadn't she? The Crybaby wasn't crying anymore. She was happy now. She seemed happy at dinner, didn't she? The Secret Keeper had been worried before they came that there were no other girls in The Family around The Crybaby's age, but The One with the Beautiful Voice seemed to get along well with her, which was a relief. He was quiet like her, sensitive.

But where was she? The Secret Keeper tried to remember her sister leaving the dinner table, but could only remember being at dinner and then being back in her room. There was something under the table, she thought, a dog or some kind of animal maybe. Though, no, that didn't seem right. And what did that have to do with her sister?

Surely she's in bed in the room she shares with The One with the Beautiful Voice. But it would be good to check, wouldn't it?

And The Baby? Where was The Baby? Her crib wasn't in the room anymore, but The Secret Keeper had taken care of her, hadn't she? Hadn't she gone back out to the forest after dinner? Hadn't she found the little torn body that they left in the woods? Hadn't she removed the stick from its abdomen and painstakingly pulled each splinter from its flesh? Hadn't she carefully placed its organs back into the spots where they belonged and, using the sewing kit she brought from home, hadn't she then carefully sewn up the wound and, for good measure, the eyes and the mouth? Hadn't she buried the body deep in the earth where the mushrooms grew in interlocking circles?

But what did all that have to do with The Baby? She was thinking in strange loops again. She tried to focus. The Baby was at dinner with her, sitting on someone's lap. She couldn't remember whose. And then someone had carried her with them when they left. When they all left, seemingly at the same time. The Baby, she thought, must be somewhere in this house. In another room, probably. With another cousin.

She should look for them. She just wanted to check, to be sure they were safe. It was the responsible thing to do.

She crept out of the room as quietly as she could, though she was surprised to see that none of her sleeping cousins woke when she had to move the creaking bookshelf away from the door. Outside of the room, the dark hallway seemed to expand a little and then contract around her. Like a throat clearing itself. It was comforting somehow. It made her feel like she wasn't alone.

As she passed each room, she peered inside to examine its inhabitants. In the largest bedroom, The Oldest and The One Who Runs Away breathed heavily, lying apart from each other on the huge mattress, the duvet cover kicked to the floor below their limp feet. The Liar and The Boy Twin had locked their old room up, so she couldn't check inside. She put her ear to the door, however. Just in case. At first, she thought there might be noises coming from inside the room, some sort of muffled conversation, but then she realized what she was hearing wasn't in the room at all, but strange words emerging from her own lips. As she realized this, she went silent. She continued down the hall.

When she entered Our Young Aunt's room, she was surprised to find the woman sitting upright on her bed. Her eyes were open, and she seemed to be staring straight at The Secret Keeper, but she didn't say anything or even raise her hand in greeting. The Secret Keeper waited for a long while, and Our Young Aunt continued staring at her blankly, occasionally moving her lips into a sort of faltering smile and then pulling them back into a grimace. The Secret Keeper backed out of the room quietly, her eyes trained on Our Young Aunt's face until she was safely in the hallway.

She passed the other double room and the other single, both quiet except for the light breath of sleeping bodies. She hovered by the doorframe of each, looking in to see who was inside. But the rooms went quiet as soon as she came close, no one to be found inside. And so she decided to check elsewhere, just to be sure.

She started with the yard. In the back of her mind, she could recall The Baby being there at some point. There was a pursuit of some kind, a chase through the woods ending at the lake. The Baby had been there, she was sure of it, running ahead of them on suddenly sturdy legs.

In the yard, she waded through the sodden grass, trying to avoid stepping on the stars there as much as possible. When she reached the front yard, she could see—through the darkness—what looked like figures sitting on the raised mound near the center, the one with the mushrooms growing in circles around it. She couldn't quite make out how many there were—four maybe. No, five. One of them seemed to spot her. It turned to her and then stood up and—as it moved—she could see that something was wrong with it. Its body wasn't like a human body. It was larger, much larger, the parts connecting in strange ways. Or perhaps they were connected the way they should be but there were too many of them together, or they were too big, or the wrong shape. She didn't like it; she didn't want to see.

She ran away.

Back inside, she felt better. Safe. She climbed the staircase, past the second floor, and up into the third. Once there, her footsteps echoed throughout the massive space, making her feel small and vulnerable. Nevertheless, she continued forward, trying her best not to look at the covered couches and chairs, which appeared—in the dark—like looming phantoms.

Toward the far end of the room, two small figures sat on the floor in a puddle of light created by a single shaded lamp, their bodies angled in her direction like they were expecting her. Her sisters.

She smiled at them, half-nervous and half-excited. She knew they had to have been around somewhere. She was relieved to have eyes on them, to have them back under her protection.

The Crybaby waved her over and she lowered herself to sit beside them. Immediately, The Baby clambered onto her lap, pressing her hot, sticky little face into her shoulder. The Secret Keeper sighed. That's better, she thought. That's how it's supposed to be.

The Crybaby scooted in closer until she was leaning on her older sister's shoulder. The Secret Keeper stroked her hair absently.

Are you two okay? she asked. *Shouldn't you be asleep by now? Does Mom know where you are?*

We're fine, The Crybaby soothed, her voice uncharacteristically calm. *Don't worry about us. We're okay, I promise. We just wanted to see you.*

I do worry, though. I'm worried all the time. None of it seems right. I think we're in danger. I think we need to leave.

As she said this, The Secret Keeper looked around and saw that the big room wasn't empty like she had originally thought. It was teeming with activity, small figures scurrying around in every corner—peering out from under the furniture, shimmying up the walls, slowly crawling toward her, their faces hidden, lowered so that they were nearly touching the ground.

She cried out and buried her face in her hands. She didn't want to see. She wanted out. She wanted everyone to leave her alone. She wanted to grab her sisters and run and run and run and never stop running until they were all safe at home.

We're okay, her younger sister repeated. *I promise. We're safe here. If you're here with us, then we can all be safe together.*

The Secret Keeper took her hands away from her face, about to respond, but her words died on her lips.

In the dim glow of the lamp, The Crybaby's face wavered and undulated. Her skin seemed loose around her features, like it wasn't her skin at all, but some other skin she was wearing like a veil over her real face. Her eyes, unmoored in flesh, seemed to float and turn in unnatural directions. She smiled, her teeth drifting slowly apart from each other as if pulled by an unseen current. Part of her seemed to be missing, but the missing part kept changing, shifting so that it was hidden from The Secret Keeper's view. When she looked at The Crybaby straight on, The Secret Keeper saw that the skin fanned out around her face like there was nothing for it to connect to in the back. But when she turned her head to the side, The Secret Keeper saw that there was indeed something there and that the lack seemed to have migrated toward her face, the space where her far eye should have been now just a torn edge.

The Secret Keeper looked away sharply and turned toward The Baby instead. The Baby was worse. There were so many holes, so many parts pierced and ripped away to expose what lay underneath, which was too terrible for The Secret Keeper to look at directly.

She closed her eyes and exhaled slowly. The Crybaby huddled in closer to her, making a small noise of sympathy. The Baby babbled quietly, nuzzling her neck and playing with her hair. When she wasn't looking at them, her sisters felt like her sisters, *sounded* like her sisters. She kept her eyes shut.

I don't know what to do, she said. To say it out loud almost made her feel a little better. Almost.

It's horrible. Everything I do just seems to make it worse.

It's okay, The Crybaby said again in that soft, calm voice that both sounded like her and didn't. *We're all safe, I promise. We can help you. You don't have to be scared. We can make it nice here, so you want to stay. I want you to stay with us, okay? We're supposed to be together. Like Mom always says.*

The Baby sweetly kissed the side of her face just like she always did when The Secret Keeper volunteered to put her to bed. She wanted to cry. She wished we were at home together, curled up on the big sofa to watch a family movie like we used to.

How? she asked. There was a part of her that knew she shouldn't ask, that she wouldn't want to hear the answer. But another part of her was so tired and so relieved to be back with her sisters. She didn't want to lose them again, no matter what they looked like when she opened her eyes.

Here, The Crybaby said. *I can get something to help you. And then you'll feel a lot, lot better and you can take care of us, okay? I can help.*

The Secret Keeper kept her hands pressed hard over her eyes. She felt silly. Her sisters were so little and yet here she was, a teenager, acting like a baby.

I'm sorry, she said quietly. *I really don't want to look. Please don't make me. I'm not ready yet. Just give me a few more minutes and then I can do it, I promise.*

You don't have to look, The Crybaby said. Her voice came from somewhere farther away in the room. The Secret Keeper listened carefully, trying to place her. It sounded like she had gone over to the corner by the entrance, maybe, where the bar cart was parked next to a stack of mirrors and framed artwork. The Baby, she noticed, had climbed off her at some point. She could hear the soft patter of her footsteps echoing throughout the room. They were joined by other footsteps, all the same, like The Baby had multiplied somehow, like she had split herself into a million different versions and they were all playing together just out of The Secret Keeper's reach.

Where are you? she called to The Crybaby, her fear spiking again.

I'm right here; don't worry.

The voice came from right in front of her. She could feel her sister's hand grasp hers. It was hot and seemed to shiver a little, but it was her sister's hand all the same.

Don't go away again, okay? she asked. *Just stay here with me, no matter what. I promise I'll open my eyes in just a minute.*

I won't go anywhere, her sister said. *And it's okay, really. You don't have to open your eyes. I have something for you. It'll help.*

The Secret Keeper felt something being placed in her free hand. It was long and thin, the faces smooth, and the edges sharp. So sharp they cut into her palm.

It's going to make it all better, The Crybaby repeated. *I promise. You won't be scared anymore.*

The Crybaby started to push the hand holding the mirror shard up to The Secret Keeper's face, but she didn't need to. The Secret Keeper was ready. She didn't want to have to do it, and she knew it would hurt, probably more than anything had hurt before, but she couldn't think of another way. She had turned over every other option in her mind, weighed them up and compared them to each other. It wasn't the first time she had done something she didn't want to do to make things better for everyone else, but at least this time there seemed to be the promise of a type of ending. A chance to rest. This was for the best. It was the only way forward.

*

Outside, The Crybaby stared up at the stars. The sky was full of them now, though they looked a bit different than they had before. Or no, it wasn't the stars that looked different, but the fabric of the space around them. Instead of smooth, inky blackness, there was a kind of texture to it. Spiky, like bits of it were pulled out into thin blades or strings. It reminded her of something, but she couldn't think of what.

Though most of her body was buried deep in the earth, a deep sense of contentment coursed through her. She had no need to pick at the skin around her nails or chew the inside of her lip. She didn't even quite know how she might go about doing these things now or where the parts necessary to perform these actions might be located. She could just be still, perhaps for the first time in her life. We all could. Without understanding how, we knew that we were everywhere, could be everywhere if and when we wanted to be, so there was no real need to move at all. The Crybaby hadn't realized this completely yet, but she was beginning to.

For now, The Crybaby was still in some of her body, the crown of her head pillowed by the soft ground. To her right, The Oldest ran and played without moving a muscle. To her left, The One with the Beautiful Voice curled up in the roots of a tree, and The Baby napped in between us. Ants crawled all over her as she slept, busying themselves about with bits of skin and fabric and connective tissue of all kinds. Such helpful creatures, The Crybaby thought vaguely. There were Others with us as well, though they were so far from what The Crybaby had been before that she had difficulty understanding them yet.

The One Who Runs Away was crouched somewhere above her head. But he wasn't turned in the same direction as the rest of us. He was on the other side, submerged in the sky. The melody he whistled seemed familiar to The Crybaby, though she couldn't place where she had heard it before. Every so often, he would press the amber liquid to her lips and she would drink from it like she was a baby again and the bottle was her mother's breast. Another figure was with us, too, but far off, sitting on the porch and smoking as he watched us all silently. He didn't speak to those of us who were in the ground, didn't even look at us. Instead, he seemed to be supervising what was happening over our bodies. Distantly, though, and without interfering, the way he did when our parents used to discipline us in his presence.

The amber liquid made The Crybaby sleepy, and so she let her eyelids droop, allowing the crimson light flooding her mind to wash over her eyes. She heard footsteps somewhere near and—when she looked up—saw The Secret Keeper walking above our heads, hand in hand with The One Who Runs Away. She was turned away from the rest of us, so The Crybaby only caught a quick glimpse of what remained of the upper part of her face. She winced a little, at the memory of having a real body, but relaxed when she remembered that her sister would rid herself of hers soon enough.

Somewhere in the sky, the bits of The Secret Keeper she had cut out of herself floated by, streaking red through the stars like an aurora. Like everything else, The Secret Keeper wouldn't need them anymore. We saw in different ways down here.

They're all sleeping right now, The Crybaby heard The One Who Runs Away say, *but you'll see them soon.*

As The One Who Runs Away led The Secret Keeper to the center of one of the circles, The Crybaby tried to crane her neck to watch, but she couldn't find the muscles and nerves she needed. Instead, she listened as they sat down in the grass and began digging together, chatting softly. She wondered if she'd be able to hear it, the moment The Secret Keeper joined us, and she knew she wouldn't, and she accepted that. She would feel it, she knew, like all of us would. We would feel it together.

*

The Liar wasn't surprised when she awoke to find The Secret Keeper gone. She had dreamt about her the night before. In her dream, The Secret Keeper sat in a clearing in the middle of the woods, surrounded by animals like a princess from a fairy tale. Each creature approached The Secret Keeper in turn and, as they did so, The Secret Keeper gave something to them. The first to approach were two foxes, and to these, The Secret Keeper gifted her eyes. The ants and beetles and other insects worked on her tongue and, once it was separated from her mouth, they passed it back to each other down a long line of tiny, organized bodies. Squirrels and chipmunks were bestowed her teeth, which they eagerly stashed away in their cheeks. A couple rabbits took off with her clothing. The deer took her nails, employing their gentle mouths and long tongues to suck them off her fingers and toes like rock candy. Her hair was taken by the birds, strand by strand, to bring back to their nests.

More creatures came out of the forest, their heads bowed in something approaching reverence. They gently opened her toothless, tongueless mouth and—as she sat patiently in the clearing, shadows of black and green and gold playing over her body—reached down with paws or beaks or webbed fingers to remove each ripe organ. At last, when the rest were through, the largest animal cast its shadow over the clearing. When it was done with her, only muscle and bone remained. She seemed to smile then, and lowered her flayed body to the ground, where it was wrapped in vines and fungus and the rich, living soil of the forest floor.

It had been a peaceful dream, almost soothing, but sad too. The Liar missed The Secret Keeper, though there was little reason for her to. They hadn't been close. The Liar was always aware that The Secret Keeper didn't like her much, didn't approve of her playing with her sisters. But she missed her anyways. Despite herself, she liked it best when we were all together.

Once The Twins were awake, the three of us made our way down to The Main House for breakfast. We held hands and kept our eyes trained on the ground in front of us, refusing to look into any of the bedrooms we passed, though they were wide open to us, the doors left ajar.

We were quiet throughout breakfast. While everyone else laughed and joked with each other over blueberry pancakes and bacon and hash browns, we focused on chewing and didn't speak at all.

What's up with you guys? The Oldest asked, bacon fat popping between his teeth.

Maybe they're tired, offered The Secret Keeper. *Did you sleep okay?*

We could feel her staring at us but still none of us spoke, though The Boy Twin looked over at his sister to check what she was doing before he continued his silent chewing.

We should do something fun today, something special, The One with the Beautiful Voice added.

Yeah, said The Crybaby. *Let's do something all together!*

Let's go to the lake, said The One Who Runs Away. We didn't look up at him when he said it, but—despite this—we could feel him staring at us, could feel him smiling.

*

If we were different—older, maybe, more used to the woods, to big empty spaces—we might have tried to escape. But we wouldn't have known where to run to or what to bring or what to say if we were found. The prospect seemed difficult and tedious and unlikely to have a good outcome. Despite how we may have wanted to, we couldn't imagine a world in which we lived in different places, with different families, doing things that were unfamiliar to us.

And so we went to the lake. To our credit, we took as much time as we could getting ready, pulling our swimsuits on inch by inch, searching through the entire Children's Wing for the towels we thought would best suit us. But eventually, we could avoid it no longer and—at The Secret Keeper's beckoning—we trudged out together to the front lawn, where we were quickly sorted into cars, driven three minutes down the road, and deposited at the mouth of the water.

It was a decently sized lake, about three city blocks across and spreading a mile or so out from the river. Only people who owned land in the area were allowed to swim in it, and so that meant it was mostly just for us. It was nearly empty when we got there, aside from a small sailboat bobbing far across on the other side and a group of middle-aged couples hanging out on a motorboat near the water's edge, laughing and whooping like teenagers. A little after we got there, they spotted us and took off to the other side.

The Boy Twin, who had only ever been swimming at beaches and pools, expected there to be sand and was a little disappointed when instead there was only a lawn that tapered off into pebbles and silt. There was a dock, though, jutting out into the water, far enough from the rocks that it was safe to jump off. The Liar and The Girl Twin still seemed subdued and troubled and, while he was abstractly aware that strange things were happening around him, he understood managing chaos to be a job for adults. One of them would handle it, he thought. If it was really a problem, then a parent would do something about it.

As the rest of us unpacked the picnic baskets on the grass and set up our towels, he dropped his things on the ground and ran over to the dock as quickly as his legs would take him, bounding across the rotting, uneven boards and then launching himself into a summersault over the water. In his excitement, he hit the lake's surface hard, at an awkward angle, the water shooting up into his mouth and nose. He emerged coughing, his sinuses stinging and his eyes bleary. When his vision finally cleared, he saw that The Oldest must have jumped in behind him and was treading water a couple feet away. He grinned at his older cousin, who he rarely spent time with but whose attention and admiration he was always desperate to earn.

Nice jump! The Oldest said. *Wanna go again?*

The Boy Twin didn't even answer, just eagerly scrabbled up the ladder to the dock. The Oldest followed him, though he hung back in the water, his hands gripping the bars of the ladder but his feet trailing out behind him in the light current.

Aren't you coming? The Boy Twin asked.

The Oldest shook his head.

I don't really know how to do anything cool, but I feel like I might be able to learn if I keep watching you. Can you dive?

The Boy Twin grinned and nodded vigorously. He was great at diving. He had spent all last summer at the pool, practicing. He could even do the high dive.

What kind should I do? he asked. *I can do regular or a swan dive or even a backwards dive if you want!*

In his peripheral vision, he could see his sister approaching the dock with The Liar. He cut his eyes away before he could make eye contact with them. If his sister tried to join, he worried, her very presence would make him feel self-conscious and stupid. And no one was quite at ease around The Liar. He liked her; he always had. It had always been easy and fun between the two of them. But people acted differently when the two were together than when The Boy Twin was by himself or with other cousins. A little suspicious in the ways that people so often are when boys and girls play together, but with something else in there as well. He could never tell if The Liar was not enough of a girl, or somehow too much of one, when he caught people watching them together. It often seemed like both were true at the same time, and this embarrassed him, both on her behalf and his own.

Just a regular dive, The Oldest said, drawing The Boy Twin out of his worry. *But it'd be cool if you could go deep. Do you think you could touch the bottom?*

The Boy Twin grinned and then took a deep breath, preparing his body to enter the water. Though he knew it would be a strange thing to try to explain to anyone, he sometimes thought of his body like a well-behaved animal companion, one entirely devoted to him. Real animals were finicky and difficult to control, of course. And other people too—his parents and sister, teachers and coaches, and especially other children. Even when they tried to listen to him, which was not often, he had difficulty making himself understood. But if he told his body to run, it would run. If he told it "run faster," it would listen and oblige. And if he told it to jump, he could almost hear it ask "how high?"

He told it to jump now, and he could feel his muscles stretch luxuriously and then snap into place as he ran the length of the dock, lifted his arms high into the dazzling summer sun, and then propelled himself into the air—his hands first, and then the rest of him following behind, not trailing but in active pursuit. His body rocketed up and up and then—like a finger beckoning "come here"—bent at the waist to plummet deep into the water, slicing through it with his hands so that it parted, allowing him to slip in with barely a splash.

Down he went, blowing a thick stream of bubbles from his nose to sink further, the water pressure building behind his ears. When he opened his eyes, it was dark all around him, though he hadn't been diving for more than a second. Craning his neck, he looked up to check the surface. It was still there, glittering some ways above him, though he thought for a moment—absurdly—that it might not be.

He dove further, and as his eyes began to adjust, he caught what he hoped was a glimpse of the bottom. Something down there was catching the light. Some mica in the rocks maybe. Or a dropped pair of sunglasses. It shone with a sort of reddish-gold color from the lake water not too far below him. He paddled toward it, though his lungs were starting to ache a little. He knew he was a strong swimmer. A little longer and he would reach it and then it would take mere seconds to bob back up to the surface. Being the first to see it, to see the bottom, would be worth it.

The glint of light at the bottom grew as he descended. At first, he was cheered by this, assuming it meant he was getting close. But despite going down so far that his ears were not simply blocked but actively beginning to hurt, he couldn't discern anything in front of him other than the red light and the darkness. When he looked up toward the surface, he saw only a glint of sun concentrated on a single point.

He adjusted his body so that it was no longer angled down toward the bottom of the lake. His lungs were starting to burn, really burn now, and he was reconsidering his commitment to reaching the bottom. He needed to breathe. Soon. He turned around and began swimming up, toward the tiny glinting sun.

After a moment, he paused. The feeling he was expecting, a buoyancy pushing him up, was entirely absent. He was still swimming hard. He looked up again. The yellow-white sun glinted steadily. But wasn't it a little rusty, a little red? Was he sure it was the sun and not the thing gleaming at him from the bottom of the lake? Could he have gotten turned around somehow?

He flipped himself upside down (or was it right side up?) and completed a few experimental strokes toward the other light. He was starting to feel a little lightheaded and, because of this, when it seemed like he might be floating up, he wasn't able to fully trust the feeling. He tried the other way again. It felt the same. He looked wildly between the two specks of light. Which one was it? As his vision started to blur, the light in one direction began to pulse and throb like it was beckoning him toward it. That must be it, he thought desperately. That must be the way. His whole body screaming for oxygen, he swam toward it.

*

When he was finally just inches away from the surface, he watched as the glimmering spot there shattered and spread out into a million pieces. He broke through right as he was on the verge of blacking out and gulped air. The sky above him was dark and the lake water seemed to thicken beneath him until only a couple of inches of liquid remained and he was lying on his back in the flooded grass, looking up at a single brilliant, crimson light.

*

We stood on the dock, looking down at the water and waiting for The Boy Twin to surface. We had seen him dive in and then, a few seconds later, had seen The Oldest run off the dock and dive after him. The Oldest had climbed out of the water moments after, far off on the shore, near where our families were setting up their picnics and lounge chairs in the grass. As he shook the lake water off himself like a dog, he grinned and gestured for us to jump in before joining in with The Others as they looked for a large fish The Crybaby claimed she saw.

Where is he? muttered The Girl Twin. *He should be up by now.*

The Liar didn't respond. She was angry at herself for letting him out of her sight, her closest friend in The Family, the only one she could talk to with real ease no matter where they were. But a part of her knew it wouldn't have mattered anyways. It seemed that The Lake House would take us all eventually. It wasn't like a predator we could avoid through cleverness or speed. No, it was slower, inevitable. Like rot.

Out of curiosity more than anything, she shouted over to The Adults that The Boy Twin had dived in and hadn't come up again.

She added a note of panic into her voice that was both real and not real at the same time. The Girl Twin looked up at her sharply, her expression difficult to read.

A voice came over the grass. It was The Twins' mother, though all The Adults had started to look the same to her.

"Don't worry, honey! He's right here! You must have missed him getting out!"

Sure enough, as she had suspected, The Boy Twin was there, just behind The One Who Runs Away, who stepped aside to reveal his younger cousin skipping rocks over the lake. The Boy Twin turned and waved. The Liar smiled grimly but didn't wave back. The Girl Twin glared.

That's not him, she said. *That's someone else.*

I know, said The Liar.

What should we do? The Girl Twin asked. *We have to do something about it.*

The Liar shook her head sadly.

I don't know, she said. *I just don't know. I'm not sure there's anything we can do.*

The Girl Twin stood, her hands balled up at her sides, a determined furrow taking root in her forehead.

There's always something you can do. If you think something isn't your problem, then you've already given up.

That was another thing her father liked to say. She stalked over to where her brother played with the rest of us. He smiled in a general sort of way at her, not the smile she had known since birth but a different one, strange on his face.

I think I left something back at the car, she said. *Can you come look for it with me?*

She knew that her real brother would have known she meant something else by this, and he might have said "I'm busy, go yourself" and the two would have spoken about it later, or he might have groaned loudly and made a whole production of grudgingly agreeing before hopping after her desperately, wanting to be let in on a secret. Instead, this version of her brother smiled that same smile she was now beginning to hate, *truly* hate, and said:

No problem! Lead the way.

Without responding or waiting for him to walk along-side her, she set off toward the cars. She didn't know what she was doing yet, but she had always been good with fixing things on the fly. This was something that needed to be fixed.

She passed the cars and walked into the woods. She could hear her brother following behind her, though his footsteps had started to drag, and his breathing was heavy and ragged. She kept walking until she felt deep enough into the woods that they would be hidden from anyone passing by on the road. She turned.

Her brother lumbered toward her. His movements seemed labored, which was unnatural to everything she knew him to be, and his jaw hung slack. He looked, she thought, even more stupid than he normally did.

What's wrong with you? she asked. Though she suspected the answer, it was a vague answer, full of mystery. She wanted specifics, certainty.

He took a long, tortured breath. When he spoke, the skin of his face wobbled loose around his jaw like an ill-fitting scarf.

It's heavy. And too light. Difficult to explain. In the begin-ning. It's hard to make it fit right at first. Easier when no one is paying attention.

His speaking voice was wet and thick.

Make what fit right? she asked. This she did know the answer to. The whole answer, she suspected. But she wanted to hear him say it anyways.

The bodies, the skin.

She watched as the flesh of his hands slipped down, pooling around his wrists like gloves.

It's best with . . . lots of people or . . . The Adults, they . . . can't see in the same way, but . . . it's hard for us . . . at the start.

Hard how?

To get used to it . . . being out on the other side . . . like this . . . It takes a bit . . . to grow into it . . .

He sat down hard on the ground. His eyes, his sister noticed, were floating around their sockets like ice cubes bobbing in a glass of water.

You're not my brother?

She had meant it to be a statement, but it came out as more of a question.

He reached out a flat hand and turned it back and forth, exactly the way The Boy Twin used to.

I am . . . and I'm not, he said finally. *I'm . . . parts of him.*

The thing's mouth opened into a kind of silent laugh. A horrible, hollow sound. The Girl Twin had to look away.

Where are the other parts? she asked, staring hard at a beetle scurrying frantically across the forest floor. Its acid-green shell glinted up at her.

The thing in front of her pulled the skin of its face back like it was tightening a ponytail, though she could only see it out of the corner of her eye.

Back . . . at the house . . . in the soil.

Is he alive?

That hand movement again. "Maybe yes, maybe no" her brother used to say when he did it. It was from some movie, probably. That's where all his jokes came from.

What's that supposed to mean? she asked.

There was a long pause as the thing laboriously got to its feet and stood for a moment, wavering slightly, before turning to lumber back toward the lake.

Everything's alive, it said, its back to her.

She scoured the ground for something heavy or sharp, preferably both, and found a flat rock the size of a hand mirror with a jagged edge. She stood.

What happens to him if he gets back the parts of himself that you stole from him? Will he be okay? Will he go back to normal?

The brother-thing continued trudging forward silently, not deigning to respond in words, but sticking out its hand to make that stupid gesture again.

(Maybe yes, maybe no.)

The Girl Twin looked down at her own free hand and saw that it was shaking with rage. Without pausing to think, she ran after it—the thing that was pretending to be her brother—and struck it hard on the head with a rock. Where it hit, his skull collapsed immediately, though it didn't seem to be a skull at all. The skin there flapped with the impact and then rippled a little and folded in on itself like a sail that had lost the wind. There seemed to be no bone, no brain, nothing inside holding the flesh together. She hit it again, on the back this time, and heard a crunching sound like dried leaves, and then the whole body shuddered and collapsed onto the ground.

Almost giddy, she jumped on top of it, pinning its arms with her knees like she would when she and her brother fought each other. The elbows flattened like paper and her knees ground hard into the rocks below. With her free hand, she grabbed a sharp-looking stick from the ground and—using the rock and the stick together—dug into its back. She was going to take it all back—the skin, the hair, the eyes, the teeth, and anything else it had that didn't belong to it.

The skin tore surprisingly easily—like tissue paper—and when it did, she had to blink her eyes against the heat that seemed to pour out of its breached body. When her vision cleared, she saw the grime of the forest floor all packed inside his skin, and something else crouched within, hiding. You have to face things head-on, she told herself. It's now or never.

That was another one of her father's sayings.

She pawed through the leaves and dirt and then she saw it, all of it, straight on. And it saw her too. And when they locked eyes, The Girl Twin couldn't find the words or images or emotions to understand any of it. Her mind reared back in uncomprehending horror and—as was suited to her helpful and assertive nature—neatly poured out of her body and into the soil, leaving the rest of herself on the ground in an elegant little heap for whomever might find use for it.

*

Back at The Lake House, or somewhere around it, or maybe somewhere under, we were all waiting. All except one.

*

The Liar watched her family dry off, pack up their things, and load them into the cars. She hadn't put much effort into hiding and, if anyone had cared to, they could have easily discovered her little spot in the boathouse, where she lay alongside the kayaks and canoes, the wood of the beams catching on her trunks and scratching her belly.

No one did, though. Not even her own mother, who was only a couple yards away from her, fretting over The Girl Twin's hair.

"Oh honey," The Liar could hear her say, "you've gotten yourself all caught up in your swimsuit. Let me just get this untangled for you, so you don't have to worry about it later. Such long, beautiful hair. Mine was like that when I was your age. Would you let me braid it for you later? I always wanted daughters so I could braid their hair like my mother used to braid mine. I mean, of course . . . well, you know what I mean . . . "

The Liar winced. The Girl Twin's distant, incurious smile told her what had happened to her cousin after she chased her brother into the woods.

The Liar wondered if her mother would notice that she had stayed behind, but she wasn't surprised when she didn't. The madness in this place didn't seem specific to any single person or location. It was wide-reaching and hard to define. She watched as the last bumper disappeared up the road and into the trees before coming out from her hiding spot.

It was beginning to get dark. There was no spectacular sunset that evening, just a gradual dimming, as if someone were slowly turning out the lights. The lake was empty and quiet. There was no one left swimming or boating or playing in the grass. Even the few houses lining the shore all seemed to be empty, their windows dark. She ran her fingers over the bracelet The One Who Runs Away had given to her the night before, tugging at the loose threads, picking at the knots. She was the only one there.

Except she wasn't. Not quite. The One Who Runs Away sat in one of the white lounge chairs out on the end of the dock, his body casting a long line of shadow over the rotting boards. The seat next to him was empty, and he patted it lightly, as if he had been waiting for her.

She crossed the length of the dock, taking her time, enjoying the feeling of her body moving through the warm summer-night air. When she slipped onto the chair beside him, The One Who Runs Away lifted his chin in greeting but didn't turn to look at her.

Long day, huh? he said. *A lot to get done.*

She nodded, though she wasn't quite sure what it was she was agreeing to.

They sat in silence for a while. The sun—which was pale, almost feeble—sank below the horizon line without fanfare or protest. The sky dropped a shade closer to black.

What did you want to show me? The Liar asked. *You said there was going to be something here that I needed to see.*

It's coming, he said. *Don't worry. You'll see.*

He fiddled with the bracelet on his wrist and then slipped it off, tucking it into his pocket. The Liar looked down at her own frayed bracelet and wondered if she should take The One Who Runs Away's action as some sort of rejection. She kept hers on. We watched together as the sky darkened enough that stars began to prick through. The Liar couldn't think of what to say.

Where are your parents? she asked finally. *Why didn't they come with you?*

She hadn't expected to say it, but it was something she had been wondering since she'd arrived.

The One Who Runs Away shifted in his seat and continued looking out over the water.

Have you noticed, he asked, *how rich the soil is here?*

The Liar didn't know what to say to this. She hadn't noticed.

I guess it does seem like a lot of stuff is growing, she said finally.

That's not it, he replied after a moment of quiet. *When a lot of things are growing, that depletes the soil. It's not the growing that makes it rich; it's the dying, the rotting. That's what makes it alive. Isn't that funny?*

They never do shit like this, he continued before she could answer. *My parents, I mean. They don't really care about family. Grandpa and my dad haven't gotten along since my dad was like my age, and I don't even really know my mom's family. They never let me be a part of things. Yours are the same, right? That's one of the reasons I'm glad we've gotten a chance to spend more time together on this trip.*

She shook her head. She had the sense that The One Who Runs Away was trying to do her some sort of favor and, while she was touched by this, she was also increasingly aware of the ways in which he had misread her. When he looked at her, he seemed to see in her a smaller version of himself. But that wasn't right. He was seeing something that wasn't there.

Not really, she said. *Mine love family. They talk about it all the time, all that kind of stuff. How they think it should be. They get mad sometimes, I think, because the three of us aren't good at it together. Not like their own families are. I think they wish it was easier for the three of us to be together. Or that they could love each other more, or me more. Or a different version of me. I'm not sure which one it is.*

And what about you? asked The One Who Runs Away. *What do you want then? Why do you like it here? Why do you want to stay so bad? I know you do. I can see it.*

The Liar shrugged. She didn't often think too hard about her own motivations. When she tried to, they crumbled away, slipped from her fingers, became lifeless. She just wanted what she wanted. She liked what she liked. And if that was a problem for other people—which it so often was—well, then that wasn't really any of her business, was it? They tried to make it her business, of course, and that was never fun and was sometimes horrible or upsetting or even painful, but it could be hard for her to take entirely seriously. It was almost as if it were all happening to a version of herself that other people had made up while she watched from a slight distance.

I like the woods, she said finally. *And the lake and the river. I like playing with all of you outside on our own and not having to worry too much about what I'm supposed to be doing or how I'm supposed to be doing it or any of that. I just like it here. I like that we're apart from The Adults and that we don't have to pretend as much. It feels nice to be left alone, to have space.*

That's nice, mused The One Who Runs Away. *But it's childish. It can't be all about what you want. You have to make sacrifices too. That's something Grandpa has been talking to me a lot about lately, and it's really starting to make sense. I guess that's part of growing up, though, and you're still pretty young. It might be hard for you to understand right now. You still have a lot to learn.*

The Liar *didn't* understand. She tried to think of what The One Who Runs Away or even Our Grandfather had sacrificed. Her mind came up empty. She couldn't think of anything that they had given up, anything of their own that they had lost. What would she give up? she wondered. What would she sacrifice for something more important than herself? It felt hard to come up with something that was hers to give.

Somewhere behind them, The Liar heard a car start. Our Grandfather was there in the parking lot, sitting in his red truck. Somehow, she hadn't seen him before.

Where is he going? she murmured, mostly to herself.

The One Who Runs Away turned to look, and together we watched him pull out of the parking lot and into the road. He locked eyes with The One Who Runs Away but, though The Liar waved at him, didn't acknowledge either of us otherwise.

Where's he going? she asked.

He doesn't stay to watch. Not after the first time. I want to at least once. The night we snuck out, I saw it a little bit but only far off and, anyways, it was dark. But I want to see. I thought you would too.

See what?

You know, I was surprised when I realized he was choosing me to help him with everything. Me, out of everyone. I never expected it since I live so far and I never see, well, any of you, really. But it also makes sense in a certain way. It's been so crazy over the past couple of days, so much going on, so much to do, that I haven't really had time to think about it. It's nice to have a moment to think, to talk. And I think what I've realized is that he sees himself in me. He knows I'm like him; I can work hard; I don't rely on anyone but myself. You know he left school when he was around my age? And look at him now. You hate school, too, right?

The Liar nodded.

Yeah, it sucks. Waste of time. You know, his parents didn't support him either, but he didn't need them. He could support himself. And I think what I admire most about him is that everything he's built for himself, it isn't just for him, it's for the whole Family. Even after doing it all on his own, he still wants to share with all of us.

But it's just the two of us left, The Liar began to protest, *the rest of us—*

Like I said, it's hard work. Not without sacrifices. But it's happened before, at least once, and see how well it turned out for everyone? Three houses right nearby, just totally wrecked, couldn't withstand the forest. And The Lake House? Like it was just built yesterday. The land around here is tricky; it's too tough, too wild for most people. You have to be really smart to find ways of working with it.

But what is he—

Shhh, he said. *Quiet. It's coming.*

The Liar followed his gaze out over the lake. Just like at The Lake House, the surface of the water was full of stars while the sky itself was nearly empty. She looked up and quickly located the deep-red light that hung over the water nearly as heavy as the moon itself. As she watched it, the few remaining stars surrounding it flickered out. The sky was nearly black, illuminated only by the brightness of the lake's surface.

And then, that crimson light—which had grown brighter and bigger and so red that it made her taste blood on the back of her tongue—flared a brilliant white and disappeared before reappearing on the surface of the lake. Somehow, she realized, she had never before noticed that it cast no reflection.

As she stared at its new reflection (or was it a reflection?), something started moving in the water beneath, causing thick-ringed ripples to spread across the surface until they smacked against the dock. The One Who Runs Away got to his feet and watched in wonder as the water parted and something emerged from the light.

At first, it was difficult for The Liar to make out what it was we were looking at. Lit from below, she caught the shape of its nostrils and the curve of its chest, but an understanding of the entire figure remained elusive to her. It wasn't until it began walking toward them that its features settled into something she understood.

It was some sort of horse, but the size wasn't right. It was bigger than a regular horse, though how much bigger, she couldn't say; its scale seemed off in the distance, particularly in how its shoulders rose above water that was at least ten feet deep, and because it seemed to be moving closer to her faster than it was actually walking. When it was finally in front of the dock, she could see that its shoulders alone must have stood higher than the first floor of a house. Its body glistened in layers sliding over each other—lake water dripping off of slick muscle and sinew that rippled in waves of different shades of ripe, red fruit; pale tendons stretching and relaxing between them; veins and arteries creeping over everything like dark vines. Throughout the sodden expanse of its body, hidden organs pulsed and fluttered like small animals. There was no skin remaining.

Or maybe there was skin. Thrown across the horse's back, just above the place where its tail would have been, was a limp pile of what might have been flesh. And in front of it, on the middle of the horse's back, was something else. A rider. But not a rider. It just looked like a person, a person missing their skin, but there were no legs at all; the trunk grew directly out of the horse's back. It seemed more like an appendage, lolling around listlessly as the horse moved. Its eyes were gone, leaving behind only sockets crusted over with scabs such a deep blood color they looked nearly as black as the night sky. An image came to her of the horse tunneling through the dirt with the rider suspended in the air above like a puppet. To her surprise, the rider opened its mouth, and a sound like a million shrieking insects filled the air. When it did this, she saw that its teeth were gone as well. Its tongue too.

Though the horse was also missing its eyes, it seemed to stare at her for a long moment. She stared back, her own eyes welling up in sympathy. And then it turned its head and nudged The One Who Runs Away on the shoulder, leaving a streak of liver-colored blood on his T-shirt. The One Who Runs Away's eyes rolled back in his head and something began happening to his skin. It seemed to loosen, to droop heavily from his body like damp clothing. But before it slid off completely, he jolted his shoulder away, and The Liar saw him reach into his pocket and grab hold of the knotted bracelet, which he held up in front of him protectively. When she saw this, she also noticed that his feet had sunk into the moldy old boards of the dock. He pulled them loose with some effort as the creature screeched and turned away from him.

The creature huffed and continued to trudge up toward the bank of the lake. The Liar didn't know if she should follow it or stay with The One Who Runs Away, who had fallen to his knees on the dock with his face in his hands. She walked over to her cousin and knelt next to him. He was muttering something quietly to himself.

What? she asked.

He went quiet. The great creature stepped onto the gravelly bank. The Liar saw that its eyes, or where its eyes would have been, all four of them, had started to run with fresh blood. An acrid metallic odor filled the air.

He told me not to look. He said he did it the first time and regretted it. He said he wished he never saw it. He said it was part of his sacrifice but it didn't have to be part of mine. He said to stay away from it, not to let it touch me . . .

The loops of the bracelet stuck out from his hands where he held them over his eyes. The Liar stood and patted him absently on the head and walked down the dock toward solid land. She paused at the end, unsure about letting her feet touch the grass. It seemed like it would change something.

In front of her, the creature trod on. It was moving, she realized, up into the woods toward The Lake House and the surrounding properties.

In that moment, standing at the end of the dock, nudging her toe against one of the disintegrating boards, The Liar felt the whole of her world narrow and converge upon the scene in front of her. Though the night was dark, the area where the horse stood seemed to glow, not with moonlight, for there was no moon that night, but with a luminescence emanating from the ground itself. It was like a picture she had seen once in a magazine of waves glowing blue and green as they broke over sand. *Phosphorescence*, that was the word she remembered. But this phosphorescence wasn't the cool plankton glow of the ocean. It was rust colored. Like dried blood, like river water, like earth.

She stepped out onto the grass and felt her foot sink in. The ground was warm, warmer than the air, and yielding in a way that felt both familiar and strange. The creature turned to her then, and she saw that it, too, was sinking into the ground. Though, not quite sinking; it was more like the ground was coming up to meet it, pulling up around its scabbed hooves, grasping onto the slick bands of muscle, like the dirt and grass had sprouted hands, fingers.

And then she saw it and she understood. The heat of the ground, the light, the life within. The Others hiding there, underneath. The rest of us. The creature strode toward her and she watched as we grabbed hold, caressing its fleshless flesh before releasing it to continue its journey toward the last of us. Our body had changed, spread, lost all of its boundaries, and yet she recognized us all the same. Of course she did. She was part of it too. We ached in places that no longer existed for her to join us.

The creature came to a stop in front of her, and The Liar looked up at its two faces and then down at our many and then back to the dock, where The One Who Runs Away stood alone, his arms wrapped around each other, holding his body close, keeping it to himself. The Liar wiggled her wrist loose from the bracelet The One Who Runs Away had given her. She tossed it carelessly onto the dock and the horse snorted and nudged its snout into her palm, and The Liar felt something that had always been too tight loosen around her and fall into our hands, where we held it gently. Just in case. It was still hers for the time being, if she chose to take it back.

The rider opened its mouth wide and called out again and, this time, The Liar heard us calling with it. Blood oozed thickly from its mouth and onto the ground where it fed us. It should have been a horrible thing to see—all raw, red, empty space—but The Liar laughed in delight and, as she did so, her teeth fell from her mouth and into her outstretched hands like heavy raindrops. Without knowing why she did so, she offered them up to the horse, who lipped them one by one from her palms like they were sugar cubes.

Now the creature smiled back. And laughed, a sound like insects rubbing their wings together in song, and when The Liar laughed again, her tongue flew from her throat and then she was so, so close to us.

But first The Liar heard a question somewhere, asking her if she was too tired, and she answered back in the same way she heard the question, saying that she was not. She couldn't imagine anymore what it might feel like to be tired. There was no longer anything to rest from, no need to retreat. She held the rider's outstretched hand and mounted the creature, and we all felt it when the creature's blood began pumping through the remains of her body, when the creature's breath filled her lungs. That was the only thing we missed about our old bodies—those brief moments when we could feel the living inside of them.

The Liar, who was no longer The Liar (who had never been The Liar at all), rode with us through the fields and forests, allowing our blood to shed into the soil where it would grow and turn into new life. Finally, the creature galloped into the drowned yard of The Lake House. Where its hooves touched the ground, the flood water retreated, flowing back into the river as if swallowed up by some great mouth. As we approached the three interlocking circles in the center, the creature paused for a moment, granting one last look back at Our Family from above, but The Liar, who could feel us calling her, welcoming her, turned away. Together, we stepped into the place where the circles met and sunk in.

Epilogue

When the trip was finally over, we watched as The Family began gathering their things, their children, and preparing to leave. Some of them were excited to go, ready to sink comfortably back into their own homes, their own lives. Some fretted about the responsibilities awaiting them when they returned. Some of them were already nostalgic for the trip they were still on.

"Let's do this again soon," they cried, pulling up their calendars and looking at dates for next year.

Their New Children continued playing in the woods up until their departure. Sometimes, we played with them. They would forget all about us once they left, but they were glad to have a few more moments playing in the earth, and we were glad to have a little longer to mourn our old bodies. To see them from a distance was strange and marvelous.

The One Who Stayed never joined in. He remained inside with The Adults or paced the grounds with Our Grandfather, discussing things that were important to the two of them. The way they talked now—referring to our new body as if it were something that belonged to them, as if it were something that could belong to anyone—made us laugh, and that laughter rippled through so many parts of our body (the dead parts, the living parts, the parts in between) that even they must have been able to hear it. If they did, they tried to hide it, which made us laugh harder. We waved to The One Who Stayed sometimes, through the trees, but he looked away.

As The Family piled into their cars, little knotted loops fell from their wrists and onto our ground so easily it was like they hadn't even realized they were wearing them. We watched them pull out of the driveway one by one, the cars growing smaller and smaller until they disappeared down the road. They would be back eventually, to claim what they thought of as theirs. They would bring others with them. But that wouldn't be for a while. Until then, we would be left alone together to do as we liked. The Lake House would rot, not all at once, but little by little each day, too slowly for anyone to notice until it was too late. The dead wood holding it together would be pulled, like we were, back into the ground, where it would join us in the endless cycles of the soil—living and dying and living and dying forever.

Acknowledgements

Thank you to my agent, Jordan Hill at New Leaf Literary. I can't believe I found you through this book and I don't know what I'd be doing right now if I hadn't. I have relied on your integrity, patience, and enviable competence throughout this entire process.

Thank you to my publisher, Amanda Manns, for your invaluable collaboration and vision. I am still a little stunned by everything that you do at Creature. How?! Working with you on *Root Rot* has been an absolute dream.

Thank you to the Blue Mountain Center for hosting me while *Root Rot* was born. You all took a chance on me when I had zero publications to my name, which is one of the greatest gifts I've ever been given. Also, wow, it sure is beautiful out there.

Thank you to Jamie, to whom this book is dedicated. My biggest cheerleader, my fiercest editor, the object of my deepest respect and admiration, and the love of my life. This book quite literally wouldn't exist without you.

Thank you to my parents, Marjorie and Keith, and my brother, Karl. To grow up surrounded by some of the smartest, funniest, most creative people I know is an incredible privilege. Your support has meant the world to me.

Thank you to Janice and Crystal, my favorite artists, who I can always count on for advice and encouragement. You inspire me every day.

Thank you to all of my amazing friends and family who have joined me in both celebration and commiseration and supported me in more ways than I can name here.

Lastly, thank you to all of my students over the years. The limitlessness of your imaginations has helped me find and push the limits of my own.

Saskia Nislow is a writer, ceramicist, and psychoanalytic training candidate based in Brooklyn, where they live with their partner and three cats. You can find Saskia at saskianislow.com or @cronebro on Instagram.

CREATURE PUBLISHING was founded on a passion for feminist discourse and horror's potential for social commentary and catharsis. Our definition of feminist horror, broad and inclusive, expands the scope of what horror can be and who can make it.